POSSESSED BY THE SURLY PILOT

HALEY TRAVIS

1

OLIVIA

Every single molecule in my body is screaming at me to get out of here.

Except I can't. I'm trapped.

I know about turbulence...in *theory*...but this much bouncing just cannot be normal. The loud ping of the "Fasten Seatbelts" sign doesn't apply to me. I haven't unbuckled mine once since I first sat down.

My seatmate returns, and I'm startled to register a huge, heavy body sinking into the chair in my peripheral vision. I glance over; it's not the teenage girl who was here before. It's a very large man who looks very pissed off. I stop staring straight ahead in blank terror and turn to take a better look at him.

Oh. My.

He's straight from a poster for some super-stylish European spy movie. Rugged. Masculine. Brooding and mysterious. Thick black hair, with a few threads of silver at the temples. Wide shoulders and...wow. I blink at how sexy his muscular, tattooed forearms are under his rolled-up shirt sleeves. With strong hands that look like they could handle absolutely anything. Handle...*me.*

Looking up, our gazes lock, and I feel like I've touched a live wire. His eyes are smoky, deep midnight blue, like the darkening sky just past sunset. Beautiful, and yet he looks downright grouchy.

If I weren't so white-knuckle terrified, I'd be fixing my hair so that such a gorgeous man didn't see me at my worst. But there's no energy to spare for that now. My eyes clench tightly shut as another jolting wave of fear hits me.

"You're stuck with me, sorry. The girl moved to sit with her aunt," he grumbles. His voice is deep and dark: it's almost unnerving coupled with that stern expression. He looks at me carefully, quickly realizing I'm a complete mess.

"Hey." His hand lands lightly on mine on the armrest. "Look at me." A shudder runs through me that has nothing to do with the turbulence. My eyes go to his, and somehow I feel steadier.

"Easy." It seems like he's trying to soften his gritty voice. "Deep breath in." I obey without even thinking. He holds up his left index finger, keeping his right hand pressed gently over mine. "And out. Blow slowly, like it's a birthday candle."

Pursing my lips, I can't believe I'm exhaling onto his finger. Something about this stunning older man makes me need to please him. I'm rewarded with a smile that looks a little out of place in the center of his scruffy, unshaven face.

"Good. Old anxiety trick. I'm Riggs." His voice is rich and dark. "I'm a pilot. I know this plane. I also know Captain Nazaroff, who's flying us today. You're safe."

We lurch to the left, my body falling into his. He wraps his arms around me, holding me close as he caresses my back. Since we're in the bulkhead row at the front, nobody can see us. It feels like we're totally alone.

"I'm Olivia. I'm so sorry—"

His strong hand slips up the back of my neck, sending all sorts of inappropriate and ill-timed sensations swirling through me as his fingers tangle in my hair. "Don't be. I'll take care of you."

I don't know which is worse, for Riggs to think I'm trembling because I'm terrified, or because I've never been held by such a sexy man before. Though really, both are true. So does it matter?

He pulls away just enough to look into my eyes. Maybe the poor guy was hoping for a quiet flight and now he's stuck with me. "Would leaning up against me help, Olivia?"

I'm already nodding. "Yeah. You're, um, warm."

He looks over his shoulder, but the flight attendants have disappeared, probably strapped in themselves. One strong hand massages my knee, and the other caresses my back, making me feel enveloped by this huge man.

"Do you always fly first class?"

I stifle a snort. "Please. This is my first flight ever. The check in lady saw how nervous I was and upgraded me so I'd have more room."

"Here." He moves the armrest up and out of the way so that I can slide closer to him.

"Thanks." It's like I'm in another world – normally I would never just cuddle up with a stranger. Yet as the plane lurches again, it feels natural to take comfort in the arms of a strong man who really does seem to think everything is fine.

"Big breath in, then blow it out slowly."

Mmm... Why do I love that commanding tone so much? Something about it makes me tingle in deep places that I've never paid any attention to. I've been told what to do and controlled my entire life, but Riggs is very different from my father's overbearing suffocation. So again, I obey without thinking.

I dip my head to exhale into the broad chest of this total stranger who is caressing me as if he already knows me. As if he's dreamed about touching me for years.

"I shouldn't be doing this," he murmurs, reading my mind. "I should stop."

"Please don't." I look up to meet his midnight eyes. "There's *something...*" I trail off, lost for words. I can almost smell the forest around him. He's definitely a mountain man.

"I feel it too." His eyes tighten. "But I shouldn't be taking advantage."

He tries to pull away, but I yank him closer. "Please. The way you're touching me... It's taking me away from all this."

"Being on a plane?"

"Being *trapped.*" I try not to moan as his arms pull me back against him. "That's why I've always been afraid of flying. You can't just step out of the plane for some fresh air and a quick walk around the block if you freak out."

Riggs nods. "Makes sense." His lips skim across my temple, making my breath catch. "Still doesn't mean I should be behaving this way with a gorgeous young girl." He pulls away again. "How old are you, Olivia?"

"Twenty-one. Why?"

His forehead falls to mine. "I'm thirty-four. So I should stop thinking these thoughts immediately."

Lightly pulling at his ear, I pretend to whisper straight into his brain. "Hello? What thoughts are in there that are so terrible?"

Riggs chuckles. Damn, I wish we were having this conversation on a nice safe couch, or in a restaurant. Or in a forest, surrounded by trees. Not thousands of feet up in the sky with nothing to hold us up.

"Dreams of finding a beautiful girl like you," he confesses, staring deeply into my eyes. "Now that I've found you, I'm going to have to find a way to keep my hands to myself, at least until we have dinner or something."

I don't know why this is pushing all of my buttons – heck, I didn't even know I had buttons to push! But my tight nipples are not due to the overly enthusiastic air conditioning in this stupid plane cabin. And my thigh muscles tightening have nothing to do with nerves.

I want this sexy man more than I've ever wanted anything in my life.

I know that a psychologist would probably say that I'm grabbing onto a lifeline of some kind since everything in my world is chaos and shambles. I don't care. I've never done anything purely for myself before, and touching Riggs, or more to the point having him touch me, feels incredible.

The way he's taking charge of the situation stirs something dark and desperate in me. A deep fantasy of wanting to be – not controlled, I've been there. *Possessed*. Yeah. I keep that whisper tucked away most of the time, but this man is pulling it out into the light.

"But I'm a damsel in distress," I whisper. "Don't you want to be my knight in shining armor?"

A deep shudder runs through him, followed by a grinding sound at the base of his throat as his eyes darken. "I can't tell if you're a total tease, or supremely innocent."

My lips press together firmly. "Definitely the second one."

I love the fire in his eyes. This man is hypnotic. He's drawing me into his orbit, and I never want to leave. Something about his woodsy, earthy energy makes me trust him.

The plane lurches again, sending me even tighter into his arms. This time Riggs doesn't even try to keep a bit of space between us. Crushing me to his chest, his lips are almost on mine. "Tell me to stop, Olivia."

"No."

His hand skims over my knee and up my thigh all the way to my hip as I turn my entire body toward his. He almost sounds angry as he growls, "If I start, I won't stop until you scream out your satisfaction to the whole damn plane."

I gasp at the intensity of his tone. Apparently Riggs has buttons that need pushing too.

I never take chances. Actually taking Beth up on her invitation to come to her birthday party in New York was the first time I'd ever done something so adventurous in my life. And now...

Stretching forward, I brush my lips against his, instantly feeling transported to another dimension.

His response is immediate. Riggs pulls me against him, shifting in his seat and slipping his hand under my shirt to roam over my fluttering stomach as our kiss becomes deep and rough.

His lips part, his warm mouth possessing mine as his tongue begins to explore. Everything starts to overheat. My muscles are melting and my skin is on fire everywhere he's touching me. All I can think of is *more*. I want more. Of him, of this incredible feeling...

For the first time in my life, I genuinely feel like I'm flying.

2

RIGGS

I've never felt so incredible...or so torn.

I should *not* be taking advantage of this beautiful goddess squirming sweetly in my arms like this. She's so innocent that she clearly has no idea how seductive she is. Porcelain skin. Long cinnamon auburn hair. Hazel eyes that make me dream of holding her hand and taking long walks together in Old Hemlock Valley.

I've missed the forest and Wolfe Mountain while I've been away. The scent of the trees and the damp earth there. Olivia makes me want to go back home. It's a strange feeling, suddenly wanting to take her out to the woods to hike and stargaze. To show her my world.

It's not just a response to her raw sexual energy. Olivia makes me feel...romantic. That's the last thing I would have expected from a seatmate on a plane. Between my natural grumpy demeanor and not naturally being a talker, I don't normally connect with people. Yet everything about this girl is different.

Our kiss deepens every second, her choked little moans

making my body twitch in response. Lust courses through my veins, making me almost forget where we are.

When I was a brand new pilot, I used to date quite a bit. But not for years. Not since I began preferring solitude. Not since I gave up on ever finding the right woman who would make me feel something more than physical heat.

Olivia already does. One smile from her and I feel like a champion. Holding her delicate body in my arms makes me feel like her protector. I want to care for her, any way she wants me to.

Right now, though, I want to dissolve her fear. My frightened girl can't stay breathless and shaking for so long. "We're leveling off," I whisper when I'm finally able to pull my mouth from hers. "See? Everything's fine."

She nods, blushing softly. "Thank you for distracting me."

"You realize it was a lot more than that, right?" My palm inches up her ribs. "The things I want to do to you, sexy girl."

Her eyes blaze. "Like what?"

My fingers drag along the bottom edge of her bra. "Like pull your shirt up and your bra down, then suck on your nipples until you moan." My voice is raspy. "But..."

She's already nodding breathlessly. "But...what?"

"*But* that would be too easy to see if the flight attendant checked on us." Slowly easing my hand down, I tease my fingertips into the waistband of her stretchy pants. "This, though... It would feel so good to touch you here."

Every time I move, I expect her to pull away. To draw a line. Yet Olivia keeps nodding, those big, bright hazel eyes locked on mine. "Yeah?"

"Yeah. To touch your hot little pussy." My hand twitches as I try to hold back. "I'd stroke your clit until you came in my arms. Would that make you feel better?"

Her lips part with a shaky breath. "Yeah. Okay."

So much for not touching her. That boundary never had a chance.

The plane lurches, sending me forward against Olivia's trembling body. "It's supposed to stop," she gasps, her bottom lip trembling. "Turbulence isn't supposed to last more than a few minutes. The website said so." Her voice is rising to a desperate squeak. "Does that mean something's wrong?"

"Not at all, gorgeous. It just happens sometimes. We're not too far from the ocean – sudden storms can appear out of nowhere this time of year."

"A *storm*?" Dammit, now I've made her even more terrified. Tears start to fill her beautiful eyes. "Are we in real danger?"

"No. Just breathe, baby. Everything's—"

The lights go out.

There are screams all around us as Captain Nazaroff reassures us over the intercom that everything is fine, and we're just a few minutes away from stable air.

Even though the lights will come back on almost immediately, I refuse to let my poor fluttering Olivia suffer for even that long. "Do you want me to make the stress go away?" I whisper urgently. "Do you want me to help you come right here in my arms?"

She's already nodding, kissing me, her slender fingers clutching at the back of my hair and around my shoulders. *Fucking hell.* No red-blooded male could possibly resist.

My hand plunges inside her pants and into her panties. Thankfully there are people shrieking all around us, or the entire plane would hear me groan as my rough fingers glide first through a dusting of silky soft hair, then against her tender skin.

I'm not kissing Olivia anymore. I'm devouring her. Bruising her lips with my hungry mouth. She gasps against me, her legs spreading to let me in. My thick middle finger slides through her crease, exploring her softest skin as she moans against me.

"You're so wet for me," I growl, my arm tightening around her. "Such a good girl. I want this tight little pussy soaking wet." Her eyes flash, and I wonder if I've gone too far. "Should I stop?"

"No," she whimpers, clutching me tightly. "Don't stop. Don't ever stop." Olivia's teeth sink into her pouty bottom lip. "I think...um... I like it when you take control."

I've been trying to ignore my erection, but there's no way that's possible now. My cock throbs in my jeans, begging for release. But my focus is completely on Olivia. Our first encounter, and, who knows, maybe her first climax with another person.

I've never met a woman so beautiful and innocent. For some reason her sweetness fills me with filthy thoughts, and the urge to make her fully understand the sexual electricity we could have together the second we were truly alone.

"Good girl. Just follow your breathing. Nice and slow." My finger drags all the way through her wet slit, and we both groan from the friction of my skin against hers. "Spread your legs a bit wider."

My heart lurches at how quickly she obeys. "Like this?"

"Yeah. Now lean back a bit. Put your pussy in my hand."

Olivia wriggles slightly, then my cupped palm is covering her sex perfectly. She trembles, but is no longer paying attention to the shaking and tension all around us. It's like we're hidden in plain sight, in our own naughty bubble.

I part her soft folds, stroking all around as she gasps.

Then my finger barely dips inside, just enough to gather her moisture before gliding it over the swollen button of flesh just above.

"Oh..." Her eyes half close, then fly back open as I stroke her again. "That feels so..."

I need to know. "Olivia, am I the first man to touch you?"

She cringes. "Well, my doctor at my annual checkup. Other than that, nobody. Ever."

My cock aches almost as much as my heart. This rush of savage lust is brand new.

"Breathe, baby." Her pussy releases a bit more wetness, enough to allow me to slip part of my thick middle finger inside while my thumb brushes back and forth against her tender button. "Hold onto me, and concentrate on that pressure deep inside you that wants to let go."

"Mmm," she whispers, snuggling against me.

Luckily her eyes are closed as the lights flicker again, the entire plane shaking around us. If I didn't personally know the pilot in the cockpit, I'd almost be nervous myself. But this need to care for Olivia, to comfort and protect her, is a rush that almost makes me feel high, even as the plane continues to lurch.

"Let go, gorgeous. Let me feel you come right into my hand."

Her voice is soft and breathy. "You... You really want to feel me come?"

Every part of my body stiffens. "If we weren't on a plane right now, angel, you'd already be riding my big, fat cock. You'd know just how much I need to feel every inch of you. Caress you, possess you, make you scream my name until you're hoarse and weak."

"Unhhh," she drawls, probably unaware that she's

thrusting her hips against me. "We would...um...we would be..."

Oh God, her innocence.

"We would be *fucking*, baby. I would ram you so hard you'd cry out at the top of your lungs. Make this hot little body of yours shake with every thrust. Then after you'd come over and over, I'd lick your pussy and devour you until you couldn't come anymore."

"Your mouth...there?" Her thumb drags against my lower lip, her half-lidded eyes heavy. "Oh*hhh*..."

When she shakes against me and starts to cry out, I swallow her squeals with a deep, soul-stirring kiss. Her climax is long, coming in slow, extended waves as she bucks and trembles. It's the most beautiful, passionate, raw moment I've ever shared.

When Olivia's hazel eyes finally blink open, she just stares up at me in surprise. The plane evens out and the turbulence ends abruptly as I slip my finger into my mouth, groaning as I taste her salty-sweet flavor. "Mmm. Now that's a delicious in-flight meal."

She blushes faintly, shyly pulling her clothes back into position. "Wow. Um. Thank you."

"I hope you don't think that was a one-time thing, Olivia. We're going to have a lot more to discuss once we're safely on the ground."

We're both so high on adrenaline from our secret encounter that we don't even mind when the captain announces that a nearby storm shifted suddenly, so we'll be diverting and landing at a smaller local airport immediately.

I've never truly believed that I could be with the same woman forever. Find someone perfect enough that it wouldn't feel like being tied down. Someone who would look past my mountain man roughness to see...well, whoever the hell the real me is.

And suddenly, it's happened. There is some sort of tether between us already. A connection. I've gone from being a man of the world to being putty in Olivia's tiny hands in just a few minutes.

I'll care for her forever. Be whatever she needs me to be. Do anything to fix her problems, as long as we end up together.

And yet...

How do I get a woman to stay with me when I won't even let myself stay in one place?

3

———

OLIVIA

This is wild. It's like I've stepped outside of myself. I've become someone else completely...someone who actually takes chances. It's still early to tell, but I think I might like this new me a lot.

After our unscheduled landing, Riggs carries both my large shoulder bag and his own. Luckily we didn't check any suitcases. He seems irritated by the crew, muttering a few curses under his breath. It sounds like this entire detour is being badly handled, but since I don't know what's normal, I'll take his word for it.

Once we're out in the arrivals area, his face returns to the deep scowl he was wearing when he first sat beside me.

It's crowded. Passengers are lining up to wait for buses to nearby hotels. Riggs consults his phone. "Those two hotels are going to be booked solid," he mutters. "It's the annual early summer festival. They're probably already busy with people coming in from out of town. And now this? Follow me."

Even though he's carrying both of our bags, I have to

hurry to keep up with his long-legged stride. "Where are we going?"

We thread our way through the crowd to a taxi stand just outside. It's interesting to watch his tight shoulders drop as soon as we're outside, breathing fresh air. Yeah, he's a mountain man through and through.

Then Riggs pulls up short. "Shit, I'm sorry, I didn't even ask. Would you rather take the bus with everyone to a hotel that's probably sold out? Or would you like to come with me, and I'll take care of you?"

Riggs wants to care for me, but wants to make sure that it's my decision? Something inside me melts. Nobody's ever really asked for my opinion before.

Dad always bosses me around, ignoring my preferences. Mom left because she was sick of his attitude. My younger sister Lisa just wants to be left alone to bake, and doesn't care what I do.

Riggs seems to care so much already, especially about my physical needs. Is that where my prickle of desire, the itch to have someone control me in a good way, is coming from? "That sounds great."

He nods, then hurries us into a cab. Following the map on his phone, he directs the driver to a motel off the highway. "This small place would be a last resort for the airline," he explains, "but the reviews say it's clean. Don't want you to be scrambling for somewhere to stay until we can get you another flight."

"Thank you." I'm slightly jealous of his casual confidence and ability to make the best of a situation so calmly. I'd be spiraling into a panic if I were alone.

In less than twenty minutes we're walking into what is probably the last available motel room for miles. I sit on the edge of the bed, then realize there's only one of them. That's actually okay. My only thought is to get back into the arms of the gorgeous man who has been so sweet to me.

Wait. That's not like me at all. How can I be nervous about the entire world, but not the hulking stranger who just brought me to a motel in the middle of nowhere?

"Sleepy?" Riggs asks, sitting beside me and taking my hand as if he'd done it a million times.

I shake my head. "I'm still too rattled."

"Why were you going to New York?"

My lips open, then shut. Should I tell him?

"None of my business, forget it," he nods gruffly.

"No, that's not..." I take a slow breath. "My father has been pushing me to go to the same pastry school he did, so that my sister and I can take over the family bakery eventually."

Riggs slides his arm around to rub my back gently. "You don't want that?"

"No way. One, I cannot work with my father. Two, well... Baking is okay, but it's not my life."

"So you were running away?"

"No. My friend Beth lives in New York. It's her birthday this weekend, and she invited me to her party, saying that it would be good for me to finally get my butt on a plane. My dream is to go to the University of North Carolina in Charlotte, but I'd have to fly back to see my little sister sometimes."

His eyes crinkle with a slight smile as Riggs moves his palm lower, still stroking my back. "This was a test flight before applying there?"

"Yeah. Well, I've already applied, but don't know if I'll get in. The acceptance letters are supposed to be coming soon." I can feel my expression falter through my attempt to smile. "I want to be an art therapist. A lot of people focus on little kids, but I think it's helpful for everyone. Drawing, even just scribbling your emotions, unlocks a unique non-verbal part of the brain."

"Smart girl." He nods. "I like that."

I can't hold back my frustrated sigh. "Dad probably won't lend me the money to get to the interview anyway, if I even make it to the next round. They want to meet with candidates personally for this program."

"So how did you afford this trip to visit your friend?"

I stifle a giggle. "Beth's mom works for the airline and transferred me a bunch of her frequent flier miles. My trip to New York and back was like thirty dollars." It was actually trickier to get Dad to let me take a few days off work, but I reminded him that I never had weekends off in high school since I was always working at the bakery. For once, the guilt trip worked.

Staring down at my hands, I barely move one toward Riggs, and he immediately takes it in his. "Dad said that he'd pay for school, but I know he meant pastry school. I know he has more than enough money, though, so I'm hoping he'll at least pay for my first year of art therapy, if I get in. But I honestly don't know now if I'll ever get on a plane again. I might take the train home."

He leans in, nuzzling the side of my neck. "That's a decision for tomorrow. You're tired. It's been a rough evening. Get comfy, and I'll hit up the vending machines for snacks, okay?"

"Sure. Thank you."

As soon as the door shuts behind him, I take a deep breath, then get up to wash my face and brush my hair, grateful for a few minutes alone to pull myself together.

Looking around, I contemplate the queen-sized bed. The baggy t-shirt and sweatpants I packed to sleep in at

Beth's don't feel right. Instead I strip down to just a thin tank top and the sweatpants, hoping it looks like casual loungewear. The outfit isn't exactly sexy, but it's skimpy enough to hopefully send a message?

Part of me wonders what the heck I'm doing. I don't even know this man. Yet he knew exactly how to keep me calm in an emergency, and now he's taking care of me without treating me like a child. He's already acting as if he really cares for me.

Do I care that we only connected because I was having an adrenaline rush of terror? Nope. Do I care that he's older, and I don't even know where he lives? Not in the least.

It feels like Riggs is what I've been needing all along. The sexual tension between us is an outlet for my anxiety. Hooking up with a guy this fast is ridiculous, yes, but I'm breathless to see what might happen next.

Riggs taps on the door gently before coming back in. Seeing me sitting in bed, his rugged face softens with a smile. He comes over with two large bags, then spreads out a tacky bright blue plastic picnic sheet covered in fire trucks.

"Limited selection at the vending machines," he explains. "But there was a food truck closing up outside, and I bribed him to stay open so a gorgeous girl could have a proper dinner after a stressful day." He winks. "Sorry about the fire trucks. Dollar store."

"This is all amazing, thank you."

"What's amazing is seeing you relaxed and cozy." He sets two ginger ales on the end table and spreads out the food. "Not much for a first date, but we kind of started this way too fast. Time to catch up?"

Wow. I appreciate that he's trying to pretend this isn't a one night stand, even though honestly that's all it might be. No matter how I look at it, that's the only answer. But strangely, I'm okay with that, even though I know better than to get my hopes up about anything more.

He takes a swig of ginger ale, then kicks off his shoes and socks. He snaps on a bedside lamp before turning off the overhead light and sitting on the bed across from me. He peels off his jacket, tossing it on the chair, giving me an incredible view of the broad line of his shoulders.

"Where do you live? And, you know...pilot from?" I ask.

He arranges the pillows so he can lounge back. "This year it's mostly a crappy apartment in Chicago, but I'll be moving soon. I own a house in Old Hemlock Valley that I sometimes rent out. I go there to work on it a few times a year. The rest of the time I bounce around a lot, working for various private jet companies."

"You *like* smaller planes?"

He chuckles at my shudder. "You don't, obviously."

I'm getting frazzled again just remembering today. "I just... The big planes have a whole bunch of people working on them. The engines are so much larger. I feel like they have a way better shot if anything goes wrong. Does that make sense?"

He nods. "Yeah, I guess. But any plane owned by any commercial airline is inspected to the same level. If you've paid a decent airline to fly you somewhere, you're pretty damn safe, Olivia."

His deep eyes sparkle. "Now – think about some of the assholes on the highway. Driving when they're angry, or drunk, or after doubling up on their cold meds because they're on their way to a job interview they can't miss. Honestly? Safer in the air."

I laugh, shaking some of the leftover tension from my body. "I don't know whether you've made me feel better about flying or worse about driving."

He comes closer and wraps an arm around me. "Just walking out the door in the morning is a risk. We can't live without taking them. So make the best choices you can, be smart and safe, and do what you need to do."

I could listen to his dark, gravelly voice forever. "Hmm. I've been pretty jumpy ever since Mom left when I was thirteen. I guess it made me realize that things can happen out of nowhere." I don't mention how it's left me feeling lost, rudderless, as if someone should be telling me what to do... but there's nobody there.

He strokes my arm. "I'm sorry."

"It's okay." I feel like I want to change the subject immediately. "If you own a house, why don't you live there?"

Uh oh. That dark, brooding look comes back, tilts his brows for a second, then clears. "It's more than a two hour drive from any airport. That's a long work commute. Plus..." He stares down at the last of the fries. "I don't want to bring you down."

"No, please. Tell me."

There's a very faint, deep grumble before he speaks again. "There was a guy I knew in high school, bit older than me, who refused to leave town to get a better job. Now he's stuck in a dead end gig, just like Dad, who couldn't move because Mom was so set in her ways. And my cousin, who..." He shakes his head. "Staying in one place for too long shrinks your entire life, 'nuff said."

I can see by the tension in his shoulders and the way his fingers twitch that the subject makes him deeply uncomfortable.

"I'm sorry." I try to lift his mood and smile brightly. "Hey, what's your favorite movie set on a plane? And don't say the one with the snakes."

We eat and enjoy the surprisingly good burgers. It really

does feel like a date. We chat about movies for a bit, and Riggs shares some funny stories about piloting private planes for strange celebrities.

We're truly bonding. The age difference doesn't matter. We're just two people who click, and want to learn all about each other.

He cleans up the wrappers and folds up the silly picnic blanket, then makes sure the curtains are tightly closed. "The most entertaining passengers are the ones who aren't famous, but think they are." He chuckles darkly. "If they're jackasses on the flight, I'll wait until they're leaving and then ask them if they're a politician's kid or something. Knock the 'influencers' and wannabe rappers down a peg."

My hand claps over my mouth to stifle the snort-laugh as I slip under the covers. Riggs shrugs. "Of course, I try to only be a jerk to people who deserve it."

"I don't think you're a jerk." He just gets grumpy around strangers. I get it. He's so huge he can't blend into a crowd, so everyone is going to notice and remember him. Awkward.

He eyes the bed, then frowns. "Anything I can do to make you more comfortable? This is a strange situation."

"I'm good."

Electricity is gathering in the tiny room, like the tension in the air before the first rumbles of thunder.

Riggs peels off his shirt and pants with no self-consciousness whatsoever. His body is so breathtaking, I can't even think in a straight line. Ripped and huge and strong and flawless. The deep grooves over his hips lead my eye straight to the enormous bulge in the front of his navy blue shorts. I snap my gaze to my hands in embarrassment.

My heart is racing as my legs press together, the ache between them becoming more urgent. The only time I've been this wet before is when Riggs was touching me on the plane.

"It's okay," he murmurs, sliding into bed next to me. "You can look."

Everything about Riggs is calm. I feel he's the kind of man who always knows what to do. I wonder if some of his steadiness might spill over onto me the closer we got. Even if I'm reading more into this than there really is, it's taking a chance that feels...*right.*

"I like the way you take care of me," I manage to whisper. "Maybe you could...keep doing that?"

His hand cups my cheek before gently kissing me, his warm lips brushing mine so softly that I have to hold back a whimper. Thick fingers dig into my hip as he gives me a shake. "Don't hold back, Olivia. I need to hear every single sound you make."

Need? Yes. It genuinely feels like Riggs needs me. Even though I don't know why, I know there's more to it than just being in the right place at the right time.

It's like we were never strangers. We were always meant to be together: we just hadn't met yet.

4

RIGGS

Physically, this feels perfect. Olivia's hot body against mine as she begs for more... Never in my life have I been so aroused, so in tune with a woman.

But she's young and at a strange crossroads in her life. A first relationship should be about love and connection and plans for a future together. How could she see a future with me when I've always steadfastly refused to be tethered to one location?

Her hand caresses my cheek, looking up at me dreamily. Olivia is definitely not the type to wander the world constantly. Especially not right now, with her heart set on school.

Maybe a quick, fast encounter will show her the ways of the world. Maybe it will teach her that taking chances and having fun feels incredible—

Yeah, right. *Maybe* I'm desperately searching for a way to justify this that doesn't make me a filthy older man taking advantage of a sweet, gorgeous girl. It kills me to do it, but I pull my body slightly away from hers.

"Olivia," I whisper, nuzzling her throat, "we need to be really honest right now."

"Oh, I'm on the pill," she murmurs.

Dammit. So much for one of the reasons I needed to force myself to wait. "That's great. But I need to make sure that you don't have any expectations."

She stares at me intently, then sputters out a giggle. "*Expectations*? This is a one night stand, Riggs. I expect it to be fun and that's all." Her words are light but her eyes are still searching for something.

No way is this a one night stand for me. Yet I don't have the words to explain this deep connection to her. Hell, I've *never* been able to explain myself to women properly.

"You don't think your first time should be with someone..." I don't quite know how to finish that sentence.

"Who is incredibly sweet and turns me on? That I click with? Yeah – and guess what, that's you." Her small white teeth sink into her perfectly puffy pink bottom lip. "If you want me to beg some more, I will."

Son of a... I've never been this hard in my life. My cock is literally aching as her hand runs down my chest, her soft, delicate skin a bit cooler than mine.

I've been a complete bastard many, many times in my life. Some call me grumpy. Grouchy. A few people have noted that I'm outright surly if the situation calls for it. And here I am, about to take something that isn't rightfully mine. We're purely victims of circumstance. I haven't put in the hours to get to know Olivia properly. It feels like I'm cheating the system, somehow.

I'd be fine with being a bastard to anyone else in the world.

Not to her, though.

Somehow I'll get through this night without having sex with her...maybe.

My body covers Olivia's as I kiss her hard and deep, loving the soft whimpers that she's finally stopped trying to muffle. "Yeah, baby," I whisper. "Moan for me. Moan when you come for me again."

She gasps as I shove her tank top up to devour her perky breasts. Her skin is so soft against my lips. Every ragged breath and shuddering flutter of her stomach makes my cock harder, but it also steels my resolve. I'm going to make her come, then we'll sleep. That's. It.

Kissing slowly down her stomach, I look up and watch her eyes as I slip off her sweatpants and underwear with a single long pull. She's eager and definitely excited.

Spreading her pale thighs, I can't contain my growl of pure lust as I gaze at her soft pink pussy. My fingers reach out to trail gently against her skin. "Gorgeous," I growl. "My perfect little angel."

After years of ignoring most people, studying Olivia is fascinating. Every murmur, every sigh. The way her eyes are half closed. The way her fingers brush tentatively through my hair as I move closer to her pussy lips, spreading her open gently.

I swear she stops breathing as my tongue meanders along her skin, exploring slowly and watching her pussy begin to flush. Kissing and licking steadily, I nudge closer to her clit without quite touching it. Then I sweep my tongue straight through her inner lips and across her button, making her gasp and shudder.

My girl is so easy to read. Every sound and twitch is burning into my memory. She likes it gentle, but sometimes craves it harder. Gradually increasing the pressure, my thick finger drags along her lips, slipping inside just a bit while I lap steadily against her clit.

Olivia's fingers tighten in my hair, pulling my mouth against her. I want to tell her that I'm already devoted to caring for her. That this is not just some fling in a cheap motel, but the start of our lives together.

I doubt she can read all that in my eyes, though. Nobody can ever read me properly. My features are too rugged to look friendly. Most people turn away, and honestly, that suits me just fine.

But this amazing girl stares directly at me, moaning and shifting her hips. "Riggs," she whispers as her entire body begins to quake. "Just a little more. Mmm...please..."

Digging in, my finger thrusts a bit deeper as my tongue laps faster against her swollen clit. Finally, I watch her climax spill through her. Her legs tighten around me as her back arches, fingers spearing my hair, nails pricking at my scalp as her lips fall open as she comes hard against my mouth.

That moaning, gasping breath sends fire up my spine.

Olivia collapses back against the bed as I lap up her juices, reveling in the taste of the most delicious, sweetest pussy in the world. She's mine. We already feel so connected. The wave of possession surges through me. I've never needed any other person in my life like I need her.

I kiss my way up to her lips, then lie beside her. She curls into my arms like her body was designed for mine. After a moment, she looks at me with a sweetly seductive smile.

"Please..." Her soft whisper is almost a purr as her fingers start to dip into the waistband of my shorts.

Mmm, this girl. "If you want it, beautiful, take it." I roll onto my back with my hands pillowed under my head, then grin at her soft giggle.

"Seriously?"

"Seriously. I need to know how much you want it, gorgeous." My breath hitches as her hand slips under, gripping the head of my cock in her delicate palm. "Stroke it," I command.

I groan as she rubs both hands gently up and down, caressing me tenderly. It feels like she's afraid to hurt me. She's driving me so wild that it's difficult to control myself, but I'm determined to fight the urge to throw her down and plunge inside her just to hear her tiny cries again.

"That's it." My voice is dark and rasping. "Use both hands. See how much you can touch at once as you move up and down."

She obeys instantly, diligently following my instructions to the letter. I study her eyes carefully, and it hits me: it isn't just that she wants to be careful and do the right thing. She wants me to tell her precisely what to do.

Well, in that case...

"Skim lightly along the skin. Then grip a bit more firmly. That's it. Run the center of your palm over the head." I shudder as she follows my every command. "Good girl."

Olivia's tiny, breathy sigh at the words makes my cock jump in her hands. *Fuck.* She really does adore the feeling of being controlled. I've heard of that helping anxiety. Yet I'd be lying to myself if I said this was just for her benefit. Every touch, every soft moan from her precious mouth is driving me insane.

"Lean closer," I growl, reaching out to stroke her hair. "Wrap those pretty lips around the tip, and slide them down as far as you can."

Her eyes sparkle mischievously as she shifts, moving down between my thighs. "Like this?"

Sweet merciful—

My hands grip the sheets as her mouth moves down, her lips pressing against the head. Her tongue darts out, licking all around before sucking me down, managing almost a third of it before she eases back.

"It's so thick," she giggles. "It's hard to get my mouth around it."

"Just wait until it's stuffed deep in your pussy, gorgeous." My voice is becoming huskier and I can't stop myself. Her eyes light up every time my tone deepens.

The sound of her airy gasp burns into my memory. "You really think I can take all this?"

Sure, why not let her think of it as a challenge. "I bet you can." Olivia sucks me down again, humming along my length. "That's it." Stroking her hair again, I resist the urge to fist it as I plunge my cock between those perfect lips. "See if you can take a bit more."

Oh sweet fuck...

My eyes roll back in my head from the combination of perfect pressure, perfect obedience, and the perfectly dazzling eyes of the beautiful girl looking up at me eagerly. She's so hungry. Not just for me, and to discover sex. She's hungry for life. For new things and experiences.

And she loves the way I need to possess her.

She can already read me. Feel the way my shaft pulses in her hand and mouth. I'm positive she's listening intently to the way my breathing is faltering. Her luscious lips release my cock for just a second.

"Please?"

Then she swallows my entire length, stroking firmly, and I'm already coming down her throat, fisting her hair as I thrust into her perfect mouth too hard. Hot streams of my come explode down her throat as she swallows eagerly, moaning happily until she's taken the last drop.

Luckily I'm on my back, or I know I would have fallen. Holding Olivia's sweet face between my palms, I watch in awe as she sucks and licks me clean. "Amazing, baby."

"Really?"

"*Hell* yeah."

She grins, clearly pleased with herself. "Okay for my first time?"

I guide her up to lie beside me. "Here's a tip, gorgeous. The most important thing about giving a great blow job is enthusiasm."

Olivia cuddles against me, her head tucking perfectly against my shoulder. I wrap the blankets around us, making sure she's toasty warm.

"You're so perfect," I murmur quietly, stroking down the center of her back. "Every single inch of you is divine, my gorgeous girl."

I really should stop calling her mine. Should stop thinking of anything but tonight.

There's no way to tell what's going to happen tomorrow. All I know for sure is that I've touched Heaven, and now that I have, I'm going to have to find a way to keep this angel in my life.

5

OLIVIA

Riggs is still asleep when I wake up, so I shower and dress quickly, leaving a note on the pillow: "Grabbing coffee. Back soon."

Luckily there is a café right next door where I can pick up coffee and breakfast sandwiches for two. The morning air is a welcome fresh breeze against my cheeks as I return to the motel.

Somehow, being with Riggs makes me feel powerful. That doesn't make sense, since I love it when he leads me and tells me exactly what to do. But he seems to roll with anything, taking stressful things in stride.

I'd love to be more like that. Beth always says that I need to stop overanalyzing with the "what-ifs" and just go with the moment, however it turns out. I've been stuck in my head my entire life. How did I suddenly change into someone who just *does* things?

I'm not the kind of girl to sleep with a stranger. Really. Maybe it was the surge of adrenaline from that horrible flight?

The more probable truth is Riggs himself. He's irritable

with everyone...except me. Quiet. Moody, sometimes. He's not some perpetually peppy guy telling me to look on the bright side. He considers all angles and makes quick, efficient decisions. He's a man who knows what he wants, and what's right.

Outside the door to our unit, I set our breakfast down on a beaten-up patio chair and call Beth.

"Hey!" she chirps. "How are you?"

"Well, I was on my way to see you, but we hit some turbulence." I quickly tell her how my plane was rerouted, and I'm now stranded in a small town.

"*You* tried to fly here?" She sounds incredulous. Wow – people really do think I'm a wimp.

I briefly explain that I met someone on the flight, and stayed with him, omitting the juicy details. There's no way I'm sharing something that I can't even process yet, not even with her.

"Hold on. A guy calmed you down during a rocky flight yesterday, and you're still with him?"

"Yeah. He's amazing."

"Wait – how did your dad even let you leave?"

I sigh. "I told him I was staying at your place for the weekend for your birthday. He doesn't remember that you've moved to New York. I might have not reminded him."

"Holy crap!" she laughs. "You've gone from quiet book nerd to wild woman overnight."

"Apparently." I lower my voice. "It feels like this guy is really good for me," I whisper. "Like he's opening doors in my mind or something. Helping me find ways to loosen up."

"That's amazing," Beth gushes. "Seriously, Olivia, I'm super happy for you!"

You know what? I'm happy for myself too, for the first

time in ages. Something about Riggs just makes me believe that everything is going to be okay, no matter what.

"I'm sorry I won't make it to your birthday party."

"No problemo," Beth laughs. "I'll eat a cupcake and do a vodka shot on your behalf."

"Perfect."

"Now you get back to that sexy man, and have the time of your life."

I hold back a giggle. "Wait a sec! I never said that he was sexy."

Her distinctive cackle takes me right back to high school. "Girl, you wouldn't still be with him if he wasn't. And from the way you hesitated, I know I'm right."

"Fine. You're a mind reader and super genius. Talk soon."

Grabbing the bag of coffee and food, I reach for the door just as it's opening. Riggs looks down at me, gloriously shirtless, wearing only faded black jeans. "You don't think I'm sexy?"

My cheeks glow with heat. "I-I didn't say that. I just..."

He laughs, taking the bag from me. "This is very sweet. Thank you."

He's already made the bed well enough that we sprawl across it for a picnic. As we eat our sandwiches and drink our coffees – no sugar and just a touch of milk for both of us – we fall into a long, meandering conversation about our lives.

Riggs is surprisingly easy to talk to, when I'm able to focus on his words instead of his broad shoulders and thick forearms. It feels like it's taking some effort for him to chat, though, as if he's not quite used to it. He's always staring into space as he chooses his words.

The age difference between us is clear when it comes to our respective life experience, yet we're fascinated with each other. My dream career path seems to interest him, and I love the way he scowls whenever I mention how demanding and nitpicky my father is.

I'm intrigued by the way Riggs moves from city to city and job to job, not really wanting a home base. Meanwhile, he's amused when I explain how Beth always tries to push me out of my comfort zone.

"That's good," he nods. "It's important to have people who support us, but give us that kick in the pants we need sometimes."

He drains the last of his coffee, then grunts as he sets it aside. "Like my buddy, Benny. He's getting pretty creative with his methods of persuading me to join his new company."

"Yeah?"

He shakes his head. "Yeah. It sounds like a great idea. 'Cufflinks Private Air' – think high class private planes, but he's found a few ways to bring the costs down a little. All of the glamor and personalized custom service, for a slightly better price."

"Cufflinks?" I smirk. He rolls his eyes.

"Stylish and filled with class – the gleaming jets and polished crew are the diamond cufflinks on the perfect suit," he intones, as if reading from a press release.

I have to wonder: do they prefer pilots with striking jawlines and gorgeous eyes? Riggs looks every inch the part of a dashing pilot. "So why haven't you agreed to sign up?"

His expression is thoughtful but unsettled as he stares into the middle distance. "I want to. But every pilot has to commit to a three-year contract. That's just..." He trails off, staring out the window to the cracked pavement of the parking lot.

"You don't want to be tied down," I say softly. "You like your nomad life just the way it is, right?"

He doesn't speak, but from the way his knuckles tighten, I feel like I've nailed it.

A tiny laugh bubbles out of me. "Talk about a pair. You don't want to be tied down, and I don't want to take chances." I smile as he finally meets my eyes. "There are already dozens of reasons why this should only be a one night thing, but that seals the deal, I think."

His strong jaw tightens as he winces. "Olivia, I don't—"

His phone rings and his eyes narrow at the name on the screen. "Sorry, I need to take this."

He steps outside, so I use the time to tidy up the room. Then I check my email out of habit. I'm not really expecting anything interesting, but there's something from my younger sister Lisa. When I see all the attachments, I switch from my phone to my laptop.

My hand flies over my mouth as I begin to shake, skimming the mail from last week that Lisa quickly scanned for me.

Riggs comes back in, hurrying to the bed as he sees my wide-eyed look. "What's wrong?"

Pointing to the screen, my hand is shaking. My throat is closed. I can't speak.

He grabs the laptop, reading the letter from the University of North Carolina. "You got in? That's amazing."

"Not quite in, but I made it to the next step." I point to the following page. "There's an in-person interview." My voice is a hoarse whisper. I honestly cannot believe what we're reading. "But I've heard it's basically a formality to check that I'm not a psycho, and have the right attitude. If I show up, I'm probably in."

"That's awesome, baby."

He turns to look into my eyes, and a wash of brand new emotions floods me. Spins my mind straight out of the equation for a moment. My breath catches as an unequivocal realization takes hold.

I want Riggs. I don't want to ever be without him.

How can I possibly think that about a man I met yesterday? It's not logical. And even if it was, it's something that I *absolutely cannot* be thinking about right now. Getting accepted to this program was the only thing I never dreamed of, and now...

Riggs tears his eyes from mine, reading the pages carefully. "Wait. The interview is at one o'clock today." He frowns, turning to me. "Why are you just hearing about this now?"

Closing the attachments, I point to my sister's cover note. "Lisa found the envelope in the trash. Dad doesn't want me to go. He wants me to work at the bakery."

"Why can't he just hire someone else?"

I snort and shake my head. "Because Lisa and I work way more hours than we're actually paid for. A 'real' employee"...I make air quotes..."would be more expensive, and he wouldn't be able to boss them around the same way."

There's a strange scratching noise. Is that Riggs' teeth grinding?

He pushes the laptop aside and takes my hands in his. "Is this what you want, Olivia?"

I refuse to let the tears that are welling up spill. "It doesn't matter. I'd never make it there in time. Even if I could beam myself there or something, I'm not prepared. When I didn't get an answer, I assumed it was a no."

"Baby." His voice is intense, even at a soft whisper. "Is this your dream?"

"It was. It doesn't matter now."

I'm yanked forward, pulled against his broad chest. "I need to hear you say it, gorgeous. If this is what you want, I'll make it happen." He pulls back again, his dusky blue eyes burning into mine. "I'll ask again. Is taking that course your dream?"

His arms around me give me the strength to be honest with myself. "Yes."

A feather-light kiss breezes along my lips. "You're going to be brave for me. And I'm going to make this happen for you." Those perfect lips tip up into a sexy grin. "Buckle up, buttercup. I'll get you there."

6

RIGGS

I don't believe in signs. Yet I've apparently been waiting for one. And now it's come.

I'd sent Benny a message last night, telling him where I was and asking if he knew any good car rental places in the area. He recommended one, then begged me again to become one of his pilots.

Until twenty minutes ago, the thought of being hand-cuffed to one boss and business for three years, no matter what, made my skin crawl. Now, as Olivia and I ride in the back of a cab to the small airfield, I feel in my bones that I'm doing the right thing.

Either that, or I'm talking myself into it because frankly I have no other choice. I can't keep floating around, taking one month contracts here and there, and living out of suitcases and storage facilities. Not anymore.

The reality is that being a nomad is only viewed as charming until a man is thirty. That said, I've never cared what people thought of me, up till now. But if I'm going to deserve Olivia, I'll need a steady job to provide a good home for us.

Just one glance from her dreamy hazel eyes and I'm helpless. No, actually – the opposite of that. Strong. Centered. Ready to be the man she needs. The safe port in the storm of her transition from living with her asshole father to being her own person in the world.

What kind of a bastard throws away a college acceptance letter? If I ever meet him, my knuckles will be flying straight through his teeth.

Deep breaths, Riggs.

Honestly? My reaction to assholes is one of the reasons it's best for me to avoid people as much as possible. The world is simpler to navigate when I'm alone. Sure, that might make me look like a curmudgeon. I've never cared.

Until now.

Squeezing Olivia's hand as we turn into the airfield, I hate how nervous she looks. The only thing that upsets me more is remembering her saying out loud that this was a one night stand. It wasn't. Isn't. Can't be. There's no way I'm letting her disappear.

Olivia seems to be in a trance as I lead us toward a gleaming white Citation Latitude with the discreet Cufflinks logo on the side.

"Can you wait here with our luggage, please?" I ask gently. "I need to go over some details. Just close your eyes and picture yourself being very calm in the interview. Okay?"

"Sure."

She seems surprised when I wrap an arm around her, kissing the top of her head. "Thinking I won't touch you in front of these people? Think again, gorgeous. I want everyone in the world to know..." I pause, hoping that my smile says what I'm sure she's not ready to hear yet. "Well, whatever we are. It's going to take some time to figure that out, right?"

Olivia nods. "Um...yeah."

My thumb traces along her bottom lip until she smiles. Then I hurry toward the mechanics and ground crew doing the checks on our plane. I know that Benny would only hire solid, qualified people, so I'm not surprised that everything is in perfect order, but inspecting the aircraft personally is something I'd enjoy even if it wasn't a legal requirement.

I'm careful to maintain a neutral expression the whole time in case Olivia is watching. The preflight checks are quick, both around the exterior of the plane and inside the cockpit. Once everything is in order, I go back out to bring in the luggage. "Showtime. Follow me."

As we step in, Olivia looks around in awe. "Wow. People actually travel like this?"

"Better. Today, *we* travel like this." I gesture to the leather easy chairs. "Would you rather sit back here, or up front with me?"

Her chin jerks up in shock. "With you? You mean...by all of the controls and stuff?"

"Yes. I'll show you how everything works, and maybe that'll make you less nervous?"

She stares down at her feet for a few seconds, then takes a slow breath. "Can I come back out here if I change my mind?"

"Of course."

I love that she's trying so hard to be brave. "Okay."

I seal the door, then gesture for her to sit in the copilot's seat. "Won't the other guy need to sit there?"

"It's just us. Benny needs this plane relocated. That's why we're getting a free flight. "

She sits down, hands plastered to her lap as if she's

afraid to touch anything. I adjust her seatbelt, then get settled myself. I casually mention everything I'm doing as I tweak and adjust things across the panels. After a moment, Olivia looks more fascinated than nervous, but remains very still, which allows me to focus on clearing the flight plan, and taxiing to the main runway.

"This plane handles like a dream," I murmur as we begin to speed up. "Deep, slow breaths, angel. I promise, I've got this."

"Okay." The word is a whispered whimper. Then she makes a tiny choked sound when the plane lifts from the ground.

"Did your stomach drop? Mine too," I say calmly. "Think of it as an exciting thrill – like a roller coaster."

"I will *never* go on a roller coaster," she whispers.

A quick glance confirms that her eyes are huge as she stares out the window. "Keep watching the size of the cars." I make sure that my request sounds like a command. "And the trees, and the buildings. Everything will shrink away and then we'll be in the clouds."

Once we've reached our cruising altitude and I've checked everything twice, my hand drops to Olivia's knee. "Weather's steady all the way there. No turbulence."

She nods, leaning slightly forward to stare out the front. "It's so different being able to see what's going on," she murmurs.

"Right? Let me show you what's happening."

A quick overview of the basic controls makes her eyes light up. "Cool! So you don't really need to steer for most of the flight?"

"No. But you can, if you want. Care to try?"

"Me?" she gasps. "I'm not qualified. I couldn't. No, that's not a good idea..."

Studying her eyes carefully, I can see she's intrigued. Nervous, yes. But she likes the idea of trying something courageous too.

Taking the controls off autopilot, I switch the guidance to her steering wheel. "It's all you now, gorgeous. Straight ahead there's a lake with lots of ducks and birds. Why don't you take us very gently to the left, so that we go around it and don't disturb them?"

Olivia is so beautiful as she bites her lip, her eyes huge. After a shaky breath, she takes hold of the controls. "For the ducks," she whispers heroically, nudging the plane a miniscule degree.

I see the change come over her. The shaky hands turning careful. The way she licks her lips, not taking her eyes off the controls. Olivia likes the power.

"A little more..." She follows my instructions beautifully, sending heat coursing through me. I'm going to win this incredible girl over, so that I can watch her come out of her shell bit by bit every single day. "Perfect. Now back to where we were before."

Olivia nods, slightly nudging us to the right until we're back on course. I switch the controls back to autopilot, and turn to smile at her. "Very good."

Her nose crinkles up adorably. "Did I really just help the ducks?"

Leaning over, I kiss her gently. "Sorry – I lied. We're way too high to interfere with any wildlife. I just wanted you to take the controls and feel the power of having this entire machine at your fingertips."

Her eyebrows knit together as she growls at me. "You... you *scoundrel*." Then she laughs. "It was incredible!"

"Glad you enjoyed. Now, review your notes and get ready to ace this interview."

"On it."

For the rest of the flight, Olivia seems to forget where we are, while I try not to get too lost in thought. I can't tell her that I just committed myself to a job for more than six months for the first time ever. Can't tell her that everything I'm feeling has already changed me.

In the tight confines of the cockpit, I have a lightbulb moment: she's the only person I've truly enjoyed close spaces with. In the front row on our first flight together. In that tiny motel room. Being so close to Olivia feels natural – even with our clothing still on.

Looking over as we start to descend, I note she still seems nervous, but is able to focus on my well-rehearsed routines as I land the plane and taxi toward the hangar.

As soon as everything is switched off, I stand and pull Olivia into my arms. "You were amazing, baby. Ready to kick some ass at your interview?"

"I think so."

After a quick steamy kiss, I release her to unlock the door. "You don't think so. You *know* so."

I flash her a grin, trying to think of something else inspiring to say, then realize I'm face to face with Benny. "I can't believe it," he laughs, clasping my hand and shaking firmly. "Finally, my buddy and ace pilot is ready to sign his life away."

I feel a dark snarl tangle my guts at the thought of it, yet desperately try to keep my expression neutral. I must have failed, because he blinks in surprise.

"Come on, Riggs. It's only three years. You're going to love flying with us. I promise."

"Sure. Right now, I need to get Olivia to her interview. Can you call us a car?"

"For sure." Benny takes off toward the office.

I turn to take Olivia's hand, and realize she is trembling. Is her fear of flying hitting her after the fact? Or is she really petrified of this interview? My poor sweet shy baby has been through a lot in the past couple of days, and here I am having to send her off to take care of this all on her own.

Grabbing the suitcases, I lead her down the steps. "Let's go to the restroom so that you can check your hair, gorgeous" I say quietly. My lips graze her ear. "Plus, I need another taste of you before you become a university student and get super busy."

Her lovely hazel eyes blaze. "Are you kidding?" she whispers.

"The first time I made you come was on a plane just a few feet from strangers. At least this time we'll be behind a locked door."

She stares at me, blinking. Then she slowly nods."If you really think it's a good idea..."

My eyes burn into hers as I stare at my breathtaking girl. "Oh, baby...I really do."

7

OLIVIA

Following a gorgeous pilot into an office in an airplane hanger is not something I could have ever imagined myself doing.

Riggs seems to think that I'm freaking out over this college interview. And I am. It's the kind of thing that I would normally have wanted a week to prepare for, not just a few hours.

But I'm honestly freaking out more over the price Riggs obviously paid for our flight. A three-year contract? He made it sound like he didn't want to do that, and then he changed his mind in a heartbeat. It can't just be for me, can it?

Riggs leads me past a few gorgeous women dressed in perfectly tailored flight attendant uniforms and into the restroom. For a split second, I feel a pang of jealousy that he'll be working with women who are so model-pretty all the time. Although he seems very eager to make a point of us being together in front of his new coworkers. Maybe I have nothing to worry about.

The door is barely locked before he pushes our bags

aside and hoists me up onto the counter. Firm lips crush mine as he grabs onto me and holds tight, his heat pulsing against me with every touch.

"This is *not* goodbye, gorgeous," he growls into my throat, nuzzling my neck. "I'm never letting you go."

My head spins. If I don't get into this university I'll have to stay at the bakery. I won't be able to live here in Charlotte and be near Riggs. Riggs, who just signed away three years of his life just to get me to the interview on time. Riggs, whom I just met. We have no idea if we're truly compatible. If we have a real chance. If these feelings are purely physical, or...more.

I have a million questions, but all I do is moan, then gasp when his hands spread my knees and run under my skirt to caress my thighs.

"I like this look. Very professional." Deep eyes burn into mine. "When you live here with me, I'm going to buy you all kinds of cute dresses."

The thought of Riggs dressing me up like a doll sends tingles through me from head to toe. I gasp as he flips up my skirt, his thick fingers pulling my panties down my legs as I press into the counter to lift my hips.

"Good girl." He slides me back against the mirror, then hooks my leg over his shoulder. "I love that you're already so wet for me."

The way his voice changes any time I'm under his control drives me wild. I can feel my pussy opening for him as I become wetter. The sensation of his tongue dragging slowly up my slit has me pressing my lips together so I don't cry out.

"Yes. Silence," he commands me with a wolfish grin, "or my new coworkers will hear you." He grins at the idea.

"Don't worry, baby. Everyone here is going to know about my smoking hot girl. But your little noises are just for me."

Riggs already makes it sound like we're in a relationship. That's impossible. Yet he's so sure that I want to allow myself to hope.

He takes control and pins me, arranging my body however he likes. As his tongue scrapes lightly over my clit, my mouth squeezes closed, terrified to make a single noise. My stifled moans come out as a faint hum, which is hopefully enough for Riggs to know that he's driving me wild.

Two thick fingers plunge into my dripping pussy, as his tongue flutters teasingly across my clit. Then he digs in, feasting on my flesh as he fingerfucks me deeply. His palm is facing up, his fingertips dragging across a strangely sensitive point that I suppose is my g-spot.

He already knows my body. Knows what I need, what I want. I always thought I'd have to travel to find adventure, and to find myself. It turns out all I needed was Riggs. My lips press together tightly as I try to stay quiet while an incredible climax builds inside me.

A palm lightly slaps my inner thigh to focus my attention. "Come for me, gorgeous. Let me feel you."

A tidal wave of heat and pleasure washes over me as my legs clamp around him. His eyes dance as he licks and strokes harder as I come apart.

"Yes," I whisper, clutching his hair as I ride his face. "Please...yes...Riggs, please..."

I don't know which I enjoy more, my own satisfaction or the glow in his eyes. When I stop shaking, he stands up, licking his lips. I try to reach for his pants, but he grabs my hand and places it on his chest.

My climax is still reverberating through my entire body, his low growl sounding like an animal about to possess its prey. It's not just the heat from our semi-secret encounter. I've never felt so much love and attention.

He pulls back, kissing my forehead. "You'll kick ass at your interview, baby. A car is already on the way."

After I straighten myself up, satisfied that I look as professional as I ever will, Riggs crushes me to his chest in a bear hug.

"Thank you," I whisper. "I don't know where to even start."

"I'm already so proud of you, Olivia." He kisses my forehead again, then gives my hips a firm squeeze. "Now go book your place in that program."

Squaring my shoulders, I walk out of the building filled with hope.

Yes, the interview is going to be terrifying. But Riggs really seems to think I can do it. He must, if he's about to sign his freedom away.

Now I have to do my part, no matter what sort of turbulence has my stomach churning.

8

RIGGS

"And this is the last one." Benny slides yet another sheet of paper into place, and I hesitate for only a few seconds before signing my name on it as well. It's been over an hour of paperwork, guidelines, rules, learning what drives the "altitude and attitude" mantra of the company, and more.

Finally I crack my knuckles and lean back. "Thanks, man."

His eyes meet mine as he nods. "I'm truly glad to have you on board, Riggs. I'm not sure why it took a girl to convince you that a steady job is the right thing, but here we are."

Grinning, I stand and shake his hand. "Great opportunity, great company, yadda yadda yadda. And you know I love the planes you've got in your fleet."

Benny chuckles. "That I do. Oh – here." He hands me a business card. "That's my Aunt Stella. She's a real estate agent, and can find you a house, apartment, whatever you want. I've already told her to give you the royal treatment."

"Thanks."

Trudging out of the office and into the mechanic's area, I find a chair where I can hide away for a few minutes. I arrange Olivia's train home, and book a car to pick her up after her interview. I'd prefer to drive her to the station myself, but it'd be too hard to say goodbye and put her on that train.

Dammit. I miss her already.

How is that even possible? Yesterday when I woke up I didn't even know who Olivia was. Now... She's like a drug that I've already become addicted to. She makes me feel complete in a way I would have not thought possible even two days ago.

I've always put a mental and emotional shield up around people. They create friction, and I'm the sort to have little patience for others at the best of times. Now I can't stand the thought of being away from this precious girl.

Looking up, I nod to the mechanic who walks by, carrying his lunchbox as he heads to a pickup truck. Looks like a nice, normal guy. Probably has a wife and kids. A home. That's what everyone is supposed to want, right?

All my life I've wanted to keep my options open because I'm terrified of the day when, against my will, those options might become limited. Then Olivia needed me to sign my life away and I did so with less than sixty seconds of hesitation.

Her future is already more important than my own. Which means that she really is the one.

This should be my dream life: flying, adventure, and a gorgeous woman to come home to. But if Olivia doesn't get into this program, what do I do? Just ask her to live with me and try again in another year?

It's one thing to hope that we'll end up living in the same city. It's quite another to suggest that she move in with me immediately. I don't even know if her father would allow that. I've noticed she gets extremely nervous whenever she mentions him. That's disturbing.

My girl is going to discover that I will always treat her like a goddess. Running a hand through my hair, I shake my head. What the hell am I even thinking? How does she know she's mine? I've never really said that outside of sex.

I check my phone for confirmations, then forward the email with the train ticket to Olivia before texting her.

Riggs: A car will be waiting outside of the main gate of the school. The driver's name is Ted. He'll take you straight to the train station.

Olivia: Oh! Thank you. I really appreciate it. They're running late, but I'm up next.

Riggs: You'll still have plenty of time to make the train home. I'll send a note to Ted to grab you a sandwich and a juice that you can have on the way.

Riggs: You're going to knock this interview out of the park. Just speak slowly, breathe calmly, and let them know how wonderful you're going to be.

Olivia: I'm so grateful for all this, Riggs. Seriously.

I want to tell her how deeply proud I am that she's jumping in with both feet. That I'm head over heels for her already. That I miss the feeling of her soft, delicate body against mine terribly. Instead—

Riggs: Kick ass, baby!

Olivia: They just called my name. Bye.

I've just finished booking a hotel room near the airport when my phone beeps.

Benny: Are you still around? If so, I have a job for you right now.

Riggs: On my way. Be there in 60 seconds.

This is what I need. Throwing myself into my new job wholeheartedly.

It's going to keep me grounded while I wait to find out if starting a relationship with the girl of my dreams is going to be a realistic endeavor, or a long distance nightmare.

Or...worst case scenario...*over,* as soon as her father catches wind of what's going on. Or when she gets into school and realizes that she'd be better off with someone her own age. Or someone more cheerful, who doesn't growl at the slightest inconvenience.

Ugh.

This whole thing began in the middle of turbulence. I don't want that to be a theme for our entire relationship.

9

OLIVIA

My bedroom feels strange when I get home. As if I've been off having adventures without any of my things...or, more precisely, without any of my baggage.

I've grown and experienced so much in the past few days that my head is still spinning.

The interview went incredibly well. They were pretty friendly when asking questions, and I think they liked my answers. They also seemed impressed by my art portfolio, which I was easily able to plug into their presentation monitor.

After the interview, as promised, Riggs had a car waiting to take me to the train station, even arranging for sandwiches, juice and a piece of carrot cake. I don't even recall telling him that was my favorite, but he must have remembered. He also sent me links to a variety of movies and podcasts for the trip. Of course I had my own list of things to keep me entertained, but having him make suggestions was incredibly thoughtful.

He's even sent me a few texts saying that he misses me,

and can't wait to see me "soon, whenever that is". He pays so much attention to giving me what I need.

So different from Dad, who has ignored me since I got home. I'm supposed to go back to work in the bakery, but honestly, I don't want to.

The work itself is pleasant enough. I love seeing customers looking so happy when they pick up their fresh bread, pies or cupcakes. Yet it was never my choice to do it. That's what paints everything with a negative hue. I was never once asked if I wanted to work at the bakery full time. Or part time, even. It was dropped on my head as soon as I turned sixteen.

Ever since Mom left, it's like Dad has wanted to keep Lisa and me under his thumb. And I hate it.

When Riggs takes control, though, it comes from a deep place of caring. Not just caring...*nurturing*. He truly wants me to be happy. My mind is still reeling from how much he's done for me.

Not just convincing me to make it to that interview. He taught me to be way less afraid of flying. That's huge! Sure, I'll still be a bit jumpy in the future, but not terrified. Hell – he actually let me touch the controls. That's *wild*.

And I can't forget the way he awakened the sexual side of myself that I'd always been nervous to tap into. With him, exploring it was effortless.

I don't know if I've ever really believed that some people are meant to be together. It's something from cheesy movies, not the real world.

Yet...*he's* real...even though I don't know yet if *we* are. Everything's happened so fast.

I finish unpacking and throw on a load of laundry, then my phone rings just as I'm plugging it in. "Hello?"

"Good evening. Is this Olivia Nelson?" The smooth, crisp female voice sounds familiar.

"Yes."

"Professor Grayson. We met this afternoon."

"Oh, yes. How are you?"

"Fine, thank you. I'm sorry to call you so late, but I like to share good news immediately. We'd like to welcome you into the program."

It's difficult not to let out a hugely unprofessional squeal, but I manage to swallow it back. "Thank you. Thank you so much!"

"You're very welcome, Olivia. We'll be emailing all of the details first thing in the morning. Have a great night."

"Thanks."

My thumb is shaking as I hit the end button. Even though I want to call Riggs right away to tell him the good news, I can barely find my voice. Rushing downstairs to the kitchen, I slowly drink a glass of water, trying to calm myself while my mind is racing.

Once the first wave of shock clears, I call Riggs, but it doesn't connect. No wonder – if he's on a flight, his phone will be in airplane mode.

> Olivia: I got in! I'm accepted! They just called! I can't believe it, and I'm losing my mind, and I don't know how I can possibly thank you!!!

"Who are you texting?"

My chin snaps up as I meet my father's cold eyes. "You don't normally giggle and grin like one of those idiotic girls," he grumbles.

It's clear that he's had a stressful day from the dangerous

set to his jaw. He's exhausted, hungry, and ready to be ticked off by *anything*. Great.

"How was your day?" I ask, ignoring the fact that he completely failed to welcome me home.

He marches over to snatch the phone from my hand. "Riggs? You've never mentioned a friend named Riggs before. What the hell kind of name is that?"

I can't stop him from scrolling back through our messages. Dad's mouth falls open. "He *misses* you? This is a boyfriend?! What the hell, Olivia – and what's this about you being accepted to college?"

Backing away slowly, I sit down at the kitchen table, trying to make myself into as small a ball as possible. "You said that if I got into college you'd pay for my first year's tuition."

His eyes burn into mine.

"I meant that I would pay for a few classes around here, preferably pastry school. You think you'll get into the University of North fucking Carolina? You couldn't even afford to fly there for the interview. And you certainly can't afford room and board in the dorms."

He scrolls through the messages again. "Wait. You already went to the interview?"

"Yes."

"And this Riggs person helped you?"

"Yes."

He steps closer and I cringe. "You've actually been whoring around with some guy just so that he would help you get into school?"

"What? No, nothing like that."

"You're not going, and that's final. You're also not seeing that kid ever again."

I feel my cheeks burn. If Dad knew that Riggs was in his thirties, he'd lose his shit. "You can't—"

His arm jerks and my phone smashes against the wall. I close my eyes, twisting away, but fragments of shattered glass nick my cheekbone, and the back of my hand. Holding my breath, I'm afraid to move.

"You're staying right here, young lady." His voice is thunder, booming straight through me. "I need you at the bakery. You *know* this. I only let you take those stupid art classes so you'd get better at decorating cakes. Now put all of that art therapy bullcrap out of your mind. I'll expect you in the shop at five am."

I can't speak, staring at fragments of plastic and glass scattered all over the kitchen. "And clean this up," he snaps before leaving the room.

My breath catches in my throat. Without that phone, I have no way to reach Riggs, and he has no way to reach me.

If I can't move to Charlotte, he'll never want to speak to me again anyway. I hate to think of what he's already given up because of me. And for nothing.

Tears fill my eyes as I grab a broom and start sweeping.

My dream of school is over, and my dream of being with Riggs is shattered all over the floor.

We can't be together.

Worse, I can't even call him to say goodbye.

10

———

RIGGS

I t was several hours before I could respond, but I know that Olivia understands that I'm unreachable while at work.

She doesn't respond, and I wait until nearly noon the next day to text again.

I'm busy most of the day looking at large apartments and

small houses, but I can't stop checking my phone. I even set Olivia's profile with a special ringtone so that I'll know when it's her. But every alert is either Benny, Stella the real estate agent, or other work contacts.

Could Olivia really have changed her mind about us? I don't want to think that for a second, but...she's young. Even though I feel like we have a deep, soul-stirring connection, I don't know all of the details of her life.

She could have gotten cold feet about me, or us, or about taking her course. Hell, she could be in some sort of trouble. I can't stop my mind from spiraling, so I try again.

> Riggs: Hey, baby. I don't know what is going on, but please send me a message so I know you're okay. It's fine if you don't want to call, but please just text? I miss you.

The rest of the day is so up and down that it would have been comical if I wasn't so worried.

Good news: Benny's Aunt Stella found me an incredible apartment in a charming building at the top of a hill so the view is unbelievable. Bad news: Olivia still hasn't messaged me.

Good news #2: Benny gets me hooked up with two regular jobs, monthly flights for a group of five business-men. I already know one of the gentlemen through previous work. This will be an easy, steady gig. Bad news #2: Olivia *still* hasn't contacted me.

The next morning I wake up and dive for my phone like a lifeline.

Nothing.

Somehow I get through the morning – sign the apart-ment lease, arrange for my stuff to be shipped, and make plans to clear out my old apartment. Then I stop by Cufflinks just to check in.

The receptionist, Brenda, jumps up as soon as she sees me. "Riggs, hi. You have a message." She looks concerned as she hands me a piece of paper. "A young woman called this morning. She was speaking very fast, as if she were trying to get off the line as quickly as possible. It sounded like she might have been in trouble."

Swallowing hard, I read Brenda's tidy printing.

Please tell Riggs that Olivia called. Dad smashed my phone, so I can't contact him. Please tell him that Dad refuses to pay for that course, so I have no way of going. And tell him that I'm really, really sorry. I hope that I can talk to him again someday.

Brenda frowns. "I tried, but I couldn't get her to elaborate. She was starting to say something else but hung up suddenly. Perhaps she was cut off?"

"Thank you." I nod, then stride angrily to my rental car.

What kind of asshole won't pay for his child's education for a very respectable job when he has the means to do so? For that matter, what kind of asshole smashes a phone, for any reason?

I need to get her out of that situation. I can't let my sweet angel live under someone's thumb like that, afraid to be herself. It sounds like he caught wind of her having a... The word *boyfriend* doesn't feel right.

I already want to be so much more than that to her.

Before I do anything drastic, I stop for a gut check. Do I suddenly want to be a provider, a partner, and a roommate all at once? Being locked into a three-year work contract is one thing. This is a whole other level of responsibility.

It's a huge decision, and at the same time not a decision at all.

It's just a plain and simple fact that is rolling over me

even as I'm grabbing my phone to start figuring out the logistics of it all.

"Someday" is not going to cut it. I need to step up and take care of my precious girl.

Now.

11

———————

OLIVIA

I'm a total mess. The past two days I've been a complete zombie.

Partly, of course, it's from yanking my schedule back to waking up so early. For me, "bright and early" is seven am, *maybe* six. Getting up at four-thirty to be at the bakery for five is not something I've ever been able to get my body clock used to.

I can already hear the peppy music inside as I turn my key in the back door. Lisa glances over her shoulder to sing out, "Good morning! The coffee is on."

Lisa, unlike me, is a morning person.

"Thanks," I mumble. After pouring myself a mug, I join her at the pastry station. I check the prep list taped to the shelf, then start making dough for the tarts. Dad is on the other side of the space, half-hidden by wire shelving as he makes bread.

"He's in a mood," Lisa whispers.

"What else is new?" I roll my eyes dramatically, making her giggle.

I've barely gotten the first batch of tart shells tucked into their pans when Dad appears at my side. "I need your keys."

I automatically dig out the ring with keys to the back door of the bakery and our house key, with a tiny metal version of Van Gogh's sunflowers attached. "Here. What for?"

He slips them in his pocket, then looks back and forth between Lisa and I, his eyes two suspicious slits. "There was a voice message on our landline. Your spot at that damn college is reserved and they want payment within the week."

"You know I don't have the money, because you don't pay us enough," I snap. "What do my keys have to do with anything?"

"I don't trust you, and you've been acting crazy." He shoots daggers at me. "For all I know, you might go into the house while I'm here and start selling things off."

My mouth falls open as I blink in shock. He shuffles back to his station, kneading another batch of dough as if everything were perfectly normal. Tears fill my eyes as I quietly go back to work. I don't have it in me to fight him today, and it wouldn't matter anyway. Even though I've saved every possible penny, I don't have enough to pay tuition and dorm fees, plus who knows what else.

"I'm so sorry," Lisa whispers. "I don't know why he's such a dick to you."

I try to force a smile. "Because I'm not obsessed with baking." She frowns, her chisel-tipped icing bag paused in mid air. "Don't get me wrong – I love that you're so into this," I say quickly. "I love that *you* love Danishes and tarts. It's just – no pun intended – not my jam."

Her eyes dart to Dad and she smiles sadly as he slides finished loaves of bread out of the oven. "*Your life is not his decision*," she says quietly. "We're going to fix this."

I appreciate that my younger sister is on my side, but it's the end of our conversation. Dad hears us talking and turns the music down a bit, so that he'll pick up every word we say.

Once the bakery is open, I breathe a sigh of relief since it means that Dad is essentially chained to the front counter. I'm still stressed, but the meditative work of baking and decorating the afternoon's cake orders actually calms me down.

"Wow," Lisa says, sliding several more sheet cakes in front of me. "I'll never be able to do lettering like that."

"Sure you will. And you're way better at the scalloped edges."

I expect her to laugh. When she doesn't, my chin jerks up. She looks absolutely terrified. I follow her gaze to the back door, where Riggs is tiptoeing in with his finger over his lips.

"It's okay," I whisper to Lisa. "I know him."

Riggs moves closer slowly, as if he's afraid to frighten me. "I tried calling the store, but I kept getting the angry dude. Let me guess – Dad?"

"Yes."

He takes my hands in his, his gorgeous midnight eyes locking on mine. "Olivia, if you're happy here, that'll be the end of it. But if you want to go to college, if you want to move with me to Charlotte, I would be honored to take care of you. I've already found a great apartment that's close to both the airfield and your school. I can transfer the funds to pay your tuition the second you give me their banking info."

"I... I can't let you do that."

"Why not? I've been saving money for years because I've had nothing worthwhile to spend it on. Suddenly I do: my girl's education for her dream career."

"I don't know what to say," I whisper. His fingers tighten around my hands, and I realize I'm trembling.

"For fuck's sakes, *do it*," Lisa hisses. "Get out of here already. Start your own life."

I glance at my sister nervously. "Can I leave you alone with him?" I tilt my head toward the front of the bakery.

She rolls her eyes, then grins. "Yeah. It'll be fine. I've never liked the guy, but he's never been an asshole to me like he is with you."

I turn back to see Riggs frowning. "Should I go speak to him, or would it be easier if we just went back to your house, grabbed your things, and took off while he's here?"

Lisa digs into her purse, pulling out a single key triumphantly. "Spare house key. Don't say I never did nothing for ya."

I slip it into my pocket. "Thank you. But what about—"

"Lisa?" Dad's voice booms down the hallway connecting the shop and the bakery. "I need you out front for ten minutes so I can start another batch of dinner rolls."

Crap. We're trapped. To make it out the back door, we'd have to cross through Dad's line of sight. "Coming!" Lisa calls out.

Riggs is already headed to the walk-in fridge. "Will we survive in there for ten minutes?"

"I think so. We might have to snuggle."

He beams, grabs an old sweater from a hook, then rushes me inside, giving her a nod. My sister grins from ear to ear. "I'll tell him you ran to the store for eggs. That always takes about fifteen minutes. I'll come back and knock on the door when he's back in the front."

Riggs and I rush into the ten foot by ten foot fridge. After the door shuts, it's pitch dark. He turns on his phone's flashlight, pointing it at the back wall, then wrapping me up tightly in the sweater. "It's not so bad in here. Although, as you say, snuggling might be wise."

I suppress a giggle as we creep to the back of the space. Because of all the shelves, we barely have enough room to squeeze together, but Riggs leans against the wall, holding me tightly against him.

"You'll really come with me?" he murmurs, rubbing up and down my back gently.

"Are you serious about paying for everything?" I asked. "That's...way too much."

"Nothing is too much for the love of my life."

Even in the dim light of the phone, I see his eyes blaze. "You heard me, Olivia. I love you. I think I loved you from the second I first looked into your magical eyes. I want to take care of you forever."

My bottom lip trembles, then he captures it in a feather light kiss.

He stops, watching my eyes carefully. "You're at a point in your life where you need to spread your wings, baby. Become your own person. I don't want to interfere with that. So if you're not ready—"

"I'm ready."

My mind is reeling. I'm about to be free of my father and the bakery. About to take the course I want to set me up for my dream job. More importantly, Riggs loves me and wants me to be with him.

The warmth in my heart makes my voice crack. "I love you, too."

"Good. Now, about those snuggles..."

His eyes glow as his rugged face ignites with a grin. Quickly untucking his t-shirt, my hands slide up his rippled abs to caress his chest.

His hand slips under my shirt, into my bra, caressing my

breast just roughly enough to make me moan softly into his lips. "Is there any chance your father might come in here right now?" His voice is almost hoarse, and I love how hungry he sounds.

"No. The dough has been proofing, and now he's quickly kneading it into ovals and flinging them into the oven."

Riggs turns us so that his back is toward the door. We're mostly hidden by the center shelf, as he fiddles with the button of my jeans. "I can't wait to get you truly alone, gorgeous," he breathes. His hand pulls away. "Damn. You're so tempting."

My giggle is muffled by his chest. Then his head dips to capture my lips, kissing me deeply. Time stops as we lose ourselves in each other. I grasp his shoulders tightly, sandwiched between the chilly wall and his hot, muscular body. I swear the man gives off more heat than the ovens just outside.

The fingers of one hand rake through my hair while his other hand trails around my breasts, teasing me perfectly. My breath stutters against his lips as I try to stay quiet.

"Olivia," he murmurs, pulling away slightly. "I swear, if you don't stop being so hot, you're gonna melt everything in here." His smile is dazzling. "Let's think about our great escape."

We shuffle my shirt back into place and I take his hand. "What happens after we get back to my house?"

"We pack up everything you want to take with you, and drive off into the sunset. Well, the sunrise, actually."

"Just like that?"

"Just like that. If that's what you want, of course."

For the first time in my life, I have absolutely no fear of going so far outside my comfort zone. "That's what I want."

He pulls my mouth against his neck before I laugh,

muffling the sound. He stiffens as the door clicks open. Then we turn to see my sister's hand waving for us to come out.

I stick my head out first, double checking the coast is clear, and toss the sweater to Lisa as I mouth the words, "I'll call you." We sneak out the back door and into a rental van.

Riggs drives to my house, and helps me pack up in record time. "Dammit," he grumbles. "I should have picked up some storage boxes on the way here. I hate putting your things in garbage bags."

"No stress." I flash him a grin as I grab the bag with my favorite pillows. "You've arranged my escape. That's all that matters."

As soon as we start driving, he hands me a paper map. "I'm appointing you navigator. We lose service occasionally on this side of the mountain, and it's a ten-hour drive, so it's safer to have an old school backup."

"Ten hours?"

"More like twelve since we'll be stopping for meal breaks, and to shake out our asses." He winks. "You don't want me to get a flat ass, do you?"

"Please. Your toned, tight ass is anything but flat. But good point. I wanna keep it that way."

Half an hour later, we're making incredible time, since the rental van has more power than he expected, even when going up the mountain slopes. I finally ask, "How did you get to me?"

"Hitched a free flight with an associate company of Cufflinks, then rented the van from a company that also has a branch near Old Hemlock Valley for the dropoff later." He shoots me a glance. "Benny's aunt is setting us up with that apartment in Charlotte that's right near your school, and close enough to the airport. But we can't move in for a while.

We can live at my house till then, and I'll drive back and forth to work."

"I hate that you'll have to commute."

"Benny understands the situation, and he's not going to schedule me too much until I'm living closer." Riggs reaches out to squeeze my hand. "In a few days I'll introduce you to a few people in town. I'm not leaving you out there alone. I've asked my friends Jace and Barrett to check in on you whenever I'm away for more than forty-eight hours. And I have a truck that you can drive into town for anything you need."

"Oh, I won't be shopping."

He shoots me a sideways glare. "Yeah, you will, using my credit card. I want you to have everything you need, and I demand that you buy it."

"I can't believe you're real."

He pats my knee. "I can't believe *you* are. Now, how about you find somewhere for us to have lunch in about two and a half hours?"

I open the map app on my phone, ignoring the multiple voicemails from Dad. It doesn't matter what he thinks anymore. He used me and controlled me, thinking only of himself.

Riggs possesses me, worships me, and has completely changed his life to create a home for us.

He's the best man I've ever had in my life.

12

RIGGS

I've always loved driving. Cars, trucks, planes, snowmobiles, you name it. This lousy rental van isn't exactly comfortable, but it's unexpectedly powerful.

Olivia is a fantastic copilot, alerting me to turns and highway changes well in advance and spacing the rest stops out according to the different kinds of food available. We spend the entire drive discussing everything under the sun, from how we'll decorate the apartment to how she's categorically forbidden to track the flights I'm on. I don't want her to worry if there's a slight delay or if things get rerouted.

I'm a guy who mostly keeps to himself, and making small talk at work is draining. Yet chatting away with Olivia is completely energizing. I've never talked with anyone so freely.

After a quick taco dinner, we hit the road again. "It looks like we're only two hours away," she says, with that sparkling grin I've come to love already.

"Sounds about right. You can nap if you like."

"No way! I'm too excited."

Waiting for a semi to pass before we merge with the

highway traffic, I'm in a similar state. Knowing that I'm finally going to have her alone, in my house, has kicked my lust for this incredible woman into overdrive. The gearshift isn't the only hard stick that I've had to control the entire day, put it that way.

After staring out at the dark landscape whooshing by for a while in silence, Olivia turns to me with a worried expression that I don't like. "Something wrong, gorgeous?"

Her fingers drum on her knee for a moment. "I guess... I'm concerned about you changing your entire life for me. I mean, we're not even really together. It's—"

"We're together."

I growl, making her spin around to stare at me as I grab her hand. "Baby, don't you think for a single second that I'll ever change my mind. This is it for me." Threading my fingers through hers, she softens. "If I don't give you everything you need, you can leave, no problem. But me, I'm in this for keeps."

"I am too." She squeezes back. "But it's a huge change for both of us. I know why I'm doing it. How about you?"

My back teeth grind. I don't want to tell her, but if I don't, she'll think up something worse.

"It's not a terrible story about my life falling apart or anything. Just a string of things. A cousin who stayed with her boyfriend who screamed at her, because she couldn't imagine finding a nicer house. A friend who fixed up an apartment just the way he liked it, and then passed on a job opportunity because he didn't want to relocate."

She nods for me to keep going.

"Dad was stuck in that horrible dead end job because there were no other options in town. I watched his soul being sucked out every single day, and he did it all for Mom."

Olivia's bottom lip starts to wobble. "And now you're doing the same thing for me."

"No. No way." I pull over to the side of the road and stop the truck, turning to face her and clasping her hands.

"Baby, this is nothing like that. First off, three years is not forever. And I'm going to be traveling all over the place." I kiss the backs of her hands. "We're going to have our apartment, and my mountain house for weekends. After you're finished school, we might relocate for whatever job you get. At that point I'll stay with Benny, or move to another airline."

Leaning over, I kiss her forehead. "Nothing is set in stone, Olivia. We're going to do what's best for both of us. Got it?"

Her lovely eyes glow. "Are you happy with your new job?"

"Once I saw the salary, and the stunning new planes..." My chuckle makes her smile. "Yeah. I really am."

"Thank goodness," she sighs. "Moving really makes sense for both of us."

I kiss her gently and start the truck again. It'll be hard not to speed to get her home. "Ready for your first look at my mountain, baby?"

"Definitely."

13

OLIVIA

When we finally roll up the long, curving driveway that feels more like a country road, Riggs seems energized, despite so many hours of driving. He's always more relaxed when he's outdoors, but as soon as we reached Wolfe Mountain, he began smiling to himself a bit.

Then the house comes into view, and I gasp.

The porch light has been left on, emitting just enough of a glow for me to see that it's a sprawling cabin-style bungalow with massive glass windows that face the valley below. Breathtaking.

As soon as we're inside and my boxes and bags dropped in the gorgeous green and gray master bedroom, Riggs takes me on a quick tour of the house. Everything is done in light wood and plush fabrics and is charmingly understated.

"During the day these windows have an incredible view of the valley." He looks down to kiss my forehead. "But now that you're here, baby, you'll always be the most incredible view of all."

I laugh as Riggs tilts my head back to nuzzle at my

throat. Our energy changes instantly. Finally, we're alone. The second his lips meet mine, our bodies press together, our hunger skyrocketing.

"Bedroom," I whisper urgently.

I'm lifted in the air before I can even blink, and he carries me down the hall. Once we're in the bedroom, he quickly lights a fire, then turns off the overhead light, switching on just a low side lamp.

It's perfect. Romantic. Cozy. Riggs reaches for me, as I snuggle into him for a soft, dreamy kiss.

My hands spread slowly across his chest, admiring every dip and swell of muscle. He is hands down the most beautiful man I've ever seen, and I know I couldn't have picked a more perfect partner for my first time.

His palm slides under my shirt, squeezing my breast gently as our kiss deepens. Moaning into his mouth, I fall onto the bed, loving his heat on top of me as he follows. I inhale sharply as he rolls my nipple between his thumb and forefinger.

He slowly pulls off my clothing, caressing every inch of my skin as his eyes wander over me. Then he stands up, quickly stripping to reveal his incredible physique. His sensual movements remind me of a panther closing in on its prey as he lies over me.

The heavy weight of his cock lands right against my mound, and my legs spread open automatically.

"I love how eager you are for me." His voice is dark and raspy. His shaft brushes against me, then he stops, his eyebrows knitting together. "Olivia, is this really your first time?"

"Yes. But I'm ready. I wanted to..." My eyes start to close as my teeth sink into my bottom lip.

"Look at me." The dark command snaps my eyes wide

open again. "You wanted to experiment with sex, but you weren't ready yet?"

"I was ready. I think. But hadn't found the right guy."

"And now you think that an older man that you just met is the right man to"...his eyes burn into mine..."give your virginity to?"

I'm already nodding eagerly. There's no way to explain how perfect he feels. How much better *I* feel when I'm around him. "Yes. A hundred times yes."

The left side of his mouth curls up in a crooked, slightly raunchy grin. "Baby, you are stunningly hot. But it's your sweetness too..." He takes my hand, placing it against his enormous shaft. I can feel his heat pulsing just beneath his skin. "You drive me crazy, baby."

That idea has a strange effect on my body. It makes me feel powerful. Seductive. Like I'm tapping into something new. Stroking his length carefully, my hand closes around the thick head. Knowing that this huge cock is going to be inside me soon has an electrical current surging through me, making my heart beat slightly off rhythm.

His lips drift across my ear. "You like what's in your hand, baby? Do you think it's all going to fit inside you?"

He chuckles as I tremble, another whimper escaping my lips. His deep blue eyes burn into mine. "I'm going to try so hard to be gentle, baby. But damn... I can't wait to fuck you deep and hear your little squeals."

Before I can gasp again, his mouth meets mine. This time the kiss takes on a life of its own. Possessive. Searching. Raw, primal, needy.

I whimper as he moves down, peppering my entire chest with sharp little kisses. When he reaches my stomach, his strong fingers pry my legs apart and I realize I'm naked, he's naked, and he's about to possess me.

Riggs pushes the blankets out of the way, then his strong, smooth hands press my knees apart. "Damn, angel." His voice is a scrape of gravel as he breathes across my open pussy, and his eyes are dark with desire as he stares up at me. "I love that I'm the first man to taste you."

"And you'll be the only one. Ever."

His massive shoulders tense, then he spreads me wider, flattening his tongue straight against my crease. I gasp, fingers twisting in the sheet as I moan, trying to hold my hips still.

Oh, my... His quick, wet tongue against my most sensitive skin drives me to a place I could never have imagined. It's past lust. Past reason. It feels like my body already belongs to him.

It's not just the physical sensations. The look of possession in his eyes. The way he controls me while seeming to worship every inch of my skin. Taken together, it's too much. My mind shuts off with an almost audible snap as my fingers thread through his hair.

His breathing changes, becoming a series of groans and growls as he laps steadily across my skin, centring on my clit. It feels like it's swelling, eager for his touch. His left hand reaches up, finding my breast and squeezing, his thumb brushing firmly across my nipple.

"You're so perfect, Olivia." The words vibrate against my clit, and another moan escapes me.

Then the tip of his tongue pushes inside, and I swear I see stars. My stomach rises and falls, twitching, and no matter how hard I try to remain still my hips begin to shift until I'm writhing against his mouth. His tongue thrusts deeper, and I quiver from the raw intimacy of what's happening. This is crazy – I just met this man, and I'm letting him do whatever he wants with me. And it all feels so perfectly *right*.

Riggs replaces his tongue with his fingers, gently stroking. Not too deep, not too fast. He finds the perfect, steady rhythm that makes me start to pull inward, the tension gathering. He places his lips against my clit, actually kissing it, then fluttering his tongue across the surface. His eyes smile as I shudder, fingers tightening in his hair as he increases the pace gradually, studying my every reaction.

"So delicious," he growls. His breathing is ragged, which thrills me to the core. "Legs up over my shoulders. Ride my face, baby. I need you to come nice and hard for me."

I obey instinctively, desperate to please him. Craving his tiny nod that tells me I've done exactly what he wanted. His rumble of approval vibrates through me as we find a rhythm, my body shifting against him. Two thick fingers enter my pussy, his tongue lapping my clit frantically.

A wave of heat floods over me like a tsunami, shaking my limbs, making my lower belly tighten as I clamp my thighs around his ears. "Riggs," I choke, crying out to the ceiling as I shake through a violent climax.

I can feel his growl against my flesh. When the orgasm fades, he smiles wickedly. "So gorgeous," he murmurs.

His eyes stare into mine, then he rubs his slight scruff of beard against my inner thigh, making me giggle before slowly kissing his way up my body. My fingers search out his shoulders...his back...everywhere I can reach to caress his warm skin.

Riggs lies over me, and I feel totally enveloped by his heat. His hands wrap around my wrists, pinning me down as he nuzzles just under my ear. My moans are loud, uneven, and I can't quite breathe all the way in.

"Easy, baby. Tell me what you need."

"You." The word is instant.

His knee presses my legs wider apart. "You want my cock here?"

As the round head of his shaft drags slowly through my wet slit, I moan shakily, watching his eyes light up. "Yes."

"Yes, what?"

His firm skin nudges against my sensitive clit, turning me to jelly. "Yes...*please.*"

Wow. The slight tremble in his shoulders tells me how much he likes it when I beg.

My teeth clench together to keep myself from crying out. I feel like a helpless damsel in distress, having a big, strong, older man care for me. Yet I've found a strength with him that I never have before. If Riggs thinks it's sexy to know how much I want him, I'll beg. I'll give him whatever he wants. Always.

"Please," I whisper breathily. "I've wanted to know what sex is like for so long. Will you..." I trail off as my hips shift, trying to pull him inside.

"Will I *what*, baby?" His voice is an even lower growl, and the look of savage lust in his eyes sends twinges chasing down my spine.

Knowing how badly he wants to possess me makes my need to be possessed ramp into overdrive. My tongue dashes across my lower lip. "Will you...um...teach me?"

He begins dragging the head across my clit and through my wet pussy lips. "Sure, baby." Our breathing becomes labored as he presses just slightly inside me, drawing out this incredible moment. "Let me guess, you feel all empty and achy inside?"

"Yeah." My hips twitch, dying to pull him in. He's hesitating. Because I'm a virgin?

"I'll make that all better for you. Now – breathe nice and slow, and try to relax. You want this?"

"Yeah. I mean... Yes, please."

"Want what, baby?"

Oh wow... I love the way he needs to hear me say it. "I want your huge, thick cock. Inside me." My lashes flutter up at him. "All of it. As deep as it'll go. Please."

"I should be a better man and wait a few weeks." He growls against my ear. "But I'm not, baby."

"You're *my* man. That's good enough."

A grinding growl tumbles from his throat. I've never felt this close with anyone before. Never felt totally at ease, yet wildly excited.

Riggs is my person. Whether it's jammed together in an airplane, trapped during a layover in a small hotel room, or here in his amazing house, it's the only thing I've ever been totally sure of.

14

RIGGS

I love the way she smiles so sweetly. Then her lovely hazel eyes turn anxious. "Unless you really want to wait?"

Kissing her hard, I move carefully, pinning her underneath me. The feeling of her soft tongue against mine, and the way my body cages her, makes Olivia feel like my precious little captive. My cock drags slowly through her wet crease, making her giggle against my lips.

"That almost tickles."

As I chuckle, I realize that Olivia has done so much more than make me more grounded and able to breathe. She's made me less grouchy. Less irritable. She's switched on a light inside me.

"I didn't know it was possible to want anyone as much as I want you, baby." Gently dragging my teeth along the side of her throat until she shivers, my shaft rubs against her clit and open wet lips. I barely nudge inside her soft pussy. "Are you sure, beautiful? You don't want me to tease you a bit longer?"

I resume dragging up and down across her clit, and her eyes become hooded as she squirms under me. "No." She looks at me intensely. "Please. *Now*."

I can't wait anymore either. Easing inside slowly, gently, I capture her lips with a long, soft kiss as I stretch her snug pussy open. She's so wet, so ready for me. Her thighs grip my hips as she tries to rock up against me. "Easy, gorgeous. Just breathe."

Olivia moans softly. "I want..."

Staring into her eyes, my grin feels wicked. A little aggressive. "What do you want?" I stop moving, barely two inches into her softness. "Tell me."

Her heel drags up the back of my thigh. "If it's going to hurt, do it quickly," she whispers. "And kiss me...please..."

I'm always going to give my beautiful angel what she needs, and if that's going to mean taking her hard...?

Her hot wet pussy is already squirming all over me as her hips refuse to stay still. "Hold onto me, baby," I murmur, before kissing her deeply.

Thrusting quickly and firmly, my cock strikes home. She gasps into my mouth as I plunge deep into her tight pussy. The feeling of opening her up for the first time sends strange possessive chills through me.

Her eyes fly wide open, never stopping kissing me even as she moans and shudders hard.

"You're mine," I growl. "This luscious body, this sexy pussy, this incredible girl. *All mine*."

"Yeah," she drawls, her eyes again half-lidded with lust. "Yours."

I love watching her come apart. Olivia is shaking, writhing, not knowing what to do with this much pent-up adrenaline. My hand grips her breast, squeezing and pinching her nipple. Her tiny squeal makes her even wetter, allowing my shaft to sink deeper.

"You need this, right, baby?" I sink to the very end of her tunnel, then we stroke and grind together slowly. "You need someone to take care of you? Someone to make this hot little body happy? To drown you in pleasure?"

"Yes," she gasps. "Riggs... You're so thick..."

"Yeah, but you need me to fill you up and let you feel everything, don't you?"

She kisses me while gasping open-mouthed, her breasts pressing against my chest. "I had no idea. Oh... It's so much..."

My hand grabs her hip, angling her body to mine, so that I'm rubbing against her clit with every stroke. Her fingers grip the back of my neck. I change from a straight thrust to a scooping one, digging deep as her eyes roll back.

"How...what..." A low erotic squeal spills from her perfect pouty lips. It's the sexiest thing I've ever heard, confirming my addiction to this incredible girl.

Her hands tighten around the back of my neck as she moves with me and against me, our heat building until our movements are frantic. The front of my hips slap against her as I thrust hard and deep and quick.

Reaching back, I unwrap her ankle from around the back of my thigh, placing it flat on the bed. Then the other leg, spreading her wide open with my bent knees. Staring down, I watch her perfect pink pussy stretched around my thick cock, wet from her juices.

From her small waist to her sexy flared hips to her round breasts bouncing with every motion, Olivia is a goddess. I feel like I've captured some sort of princess and dragged her home with me, like a savage caveman. I want to pound my fists against my chest, roaring to the world that I've won her affection.

"You're fucking breathtaking," I growl, staring at her delicate skin as she pants, her body wrenching from the force of my thrusts. Her back arches as she moans, digging her heels into the bed as her hips buck up to meet mine. I'll never get enough of her quivering, sexy body underneath me. Never get enough of those breathless gasps, her wide-eyed wonder as I worship her.

It strikes me like a lightning bolt. *I want her forever.* She's the first woman I've ever been with where I don't see an expiration date. I want Olivia completely forever and beyond.

I can feel my cock thickening even more, as Olivia writhes frantically. "So big," she gasps, her soft tits pressing into my chest again as I lean forward to kiss her. "Am I supposed to feel this full?"

"Yes. You're such a tiny little sexy thing. Your man's going to be nice and big inside you, isn't he? You want more?"

She smiles seductively, fluttering her eyelashes as she murmurs, "Yes. Please."

Damn, this girl. I can already feel the familiar tugging in my balls, as my body begs for release.

Hell no. Not yet.

She's so tight that I have to slow down a bit, wanting to be sure I touch every single nerve inside her. Her fingernails are probably leaving marks on my skin where she is clutching me. Good.

"Riggs?" Her eyes are wide and glassy, her bottom lip trembling. "I'm...I'm going to..."

Scooping an arm under her, I hold her quivering body against mine, kneeling up slightly so that I can plunge deep and slow. "Let go for me, angel. Let me feel you come."

I can already feel her tensing, my skin feverish from the heat we're creating. Staring into her eyes, I grind the base of my cock against her clit with every deep stroke as I feel the release getting ready to uncoil in her body.

"R-R-Riggs," she stutters. "Oh, yes...please...just a little more..."

The way she begs so sweetly tightens my shoulders, my spine. Even though I'm pounding her so hard I'm worried I might hurt her, the look in her eyes tells me that this is what she needs. The feeling of giving up control to me. Being captured. Being mine.

I can feel her silky walls clenching and rippling all around my cock. Olivia screams into my mouth as she comes, shuddering, exploding, falling apart. My muscles flex against her, gripping her harder, my kiss bruising her lips as we pound and reel together.

This beautiful, aching pleasure is more sensation that I've ever felt in my life. It's like being high. Ten times better than the first time I flew a plane, and that was one of the highlights of my life.

Just as I'm wondering if I can stave off my climax for another thirty seconds, Olivia presses the soles of her feet into the bed, pushing herself up and down my cock faster. She whimpers, the echoes of her orgasm still making her snug, wet pussy spasm.

Her complete surrender to me steals the last of my self-control. Pounding harder, deeper, faster, I clutch Olivia against me, kissing her savagely as hot bursts of my come spill deep inside her.

My hand grips her ass, holding her steady as I grind, smashing her lips to mine as we shake together. Finally we stop kissing, our foreheads pressed together, my cock still throbbing inside her twitching pussy.

"I love you," she whispers. "I won't tie you down, though. I'll move with you anywhere you need to go."

My lips crush hers in a ferocious kiss that leaves us both breathless. "I love you, angel," I finally say, pulling back to look deep in her eyes. "Hearing you say that means the world to me."

Moving to the side, I cuddle her in my arms. "We're going to grow together. In our first apartment for now, with me at my new job and you busy with your new school. Then we'll take it from there."

Olivia stares up at the ceiling, her eyes still dazed. "This is an incredible house. Maybe visits here can be our reward for working so hard?"

"Great idea. I rent the place out sometimes, but that can be planned around our schedule of when we want it."

Her soft smile is radiant. "I still can't believe that having the nerve to step onto a plane led me to you."

"I'm just glad that I didn't ignore my seatmate like I usually do." My lips brush the tip of her nose. "Caring for you makes me even happier than flying, you know that?"

Her hand wanders down my chest, then quickly darts to grab my ass firmly. "What about possessing me like you just did? I hope that makes you happy, too."

My dark chuckle echoes around us. "Oh baby, there are no words for what just happened. And that was just the beginning." My rough palm drags along her hip, her thigh. "A grumpy jackass mountain man isn't supposed to end up with an angel."

"A trapped baker's daughter isn't supposed to end up with a gorgeous hunk of a pilot, either, but here we are."

Rocking her gently, our breathing slows down as fatigue from the long day starts to wash over us. Olivia's fingers settle against my shoulders, her head tucking perfectly into my shoulder in a position I know we'll be sleeping in for decades to come.

"Yes indeed. Here we are."

EPILOGUE ONE
OLIVIA

** Six Months Later **

My life has been turned upside down and inside out, and I'm loving every single minute of it.

Staring out at the glorious forest on Wolfe Mountain, I deeply breathe in the clear, crisp air and the fragrance of pine.

Spending most of our time in Charlotte is amazing – Riggs is gone several days a week, but I'm super busy with school and do most of my work when he's away. Our apartment is fairly minimalist, and that's fine. Every other weekend or so, Riggs drives us out to Old Hemlock Valley to stay at this unbelievable house in the forest.

As we pull into the driveway, I still can't believe that he didn't want to settle down here from the beginning. His mountain place is so beautiful.

I jump slightly at the sound of a motorcycle, turning to see someone coasting toward the truck.

"Hey," Riggs calls out. "Cutting it kinda close there, buddy."

The big man pulls off his helmet, and I wave to Riggs' old friend Jace Wolfe, who lives around here. He's part of the family who owns a lot of land across this mountain. I don't know much more than that since he doesn't open up on the rare occasions when I run into him.

Jace ignores Riggs' scowl, since my sweetie's eyes are twinkling. "Sorry, man. I was hoping to be gone already."

"That's fine. Thanks a lot."

"No problem. Have a good one." They fist bump through the open window, then Jace yanks on his helmet and careens off as if he's in a hurry.

"What was he doing here?" I ask as we get out of the truck, and Riggs grabs our bags.

He tosses them onto the front porch bench, then takes my hand. "Nothing." His poker face slips as the corner of his lip curls up while he tries to hide a smile behind one of his trademark scowls. By now, I can see right through him. He's amused about something.

Riggs leads me around to the back of the porch, where a row of candles are lit. There's also a silver dish in front of them. "What's that?"

He chuckles. "Why don't you go take a look."

I step forward, noticing the ice bucket of champagne and two glasses on the bench.

Inside the dish, its reflections sparkling around the silver curves, is a diamond and emerald ring. My hand is trembling as I pick it up, then I spin to see Riggs on his knees behind me.

He takes my shaking hands and slips the ring onto my finger.

"I love you, Olivia. You make me a better man in every way. More grounded. *Way* less grouchy. More open-minded, too." His deep eyes are filled with such warmth. "Since this house is too far from your school and my work, I think it's time to buy a house in Charlotte. Will you marry me, so that we're not shacking up anymore?"

My high-pitched squeak isn't a proper answer, so I clear my throat as I nod madly. "Yes!"

Riggs leaps to his feet, hauling me to his chest as he spins me around. Then he plops onto the porch bench, sitting me on his lap as I lift my hand to stare at the ring.

"I noticed most of your artwork has a lot of green in it," he murmurs. "And I know you love the forest."

"It's beautiful. It's so me. No, so *us*."

He squeezes me tightly, nuzzling at my throat. "We're going to be us forever, baby."

My hand runs through his hair. "And you won't mind being tied down? Living in one place?"

"As long as I'm with my sweet girl, I'll be wherever you want, gorgeous...and I won't mind it at all."

EPILOGUE TWO
RIGGS

** Two Years Later **

Leaning in the door frame, I watch as my lovely wife fusses with her bra straps. Olivia's luscious figure, naked except for the few scraps of dark gray lace, makes my mouth water and my cock thicken. "Need some help?" I grin.

She turns to grin back. "Are you here to help me or distract me?"

A low growl rumbles in my throat as I stride into the walk-in closet. The beautiful house we moved into last year during Olivia's summer break is incredible, but it's so big that I always feel she's too far away from me.

My lips dance along the side of her throat as I slip off her bra, covering her breasts with my palms instead. "I did everything in my power not to distract you while you were studying. Now that you're done I get you all to myself."

"We're going to be late for dinner," she giggles, already shaking her hips. "What if we lose our table?"

"They'll wait."

I don't tell her that the entire restaurant is reserved for us, and we cannot get there early because that would ruin the surprise of Lisa, Beth, and a bunch of Olivia's college friends all waiting for us. After a month of screwing Olivia senseless on a variety of beaches over the course of our three-week honeymoon, I want to make sure our return to real life starts with a bang.

Literally.

Olivia moans softly, her breath already growing ragged as my hands slip down her sides, pushing her panties down so she can step out of them.

Her exquisite skin practically glows from her slight tan, her beautiful hazel eyes dancing as she squints saucily at me, her rosy lips quirked up in a naughty smile. "I *just* did my hair. You're not going to give me bedhead, are you?"

I twirl a cinnamon tendril between my fingers. "I wouldn't dare, lovely wife."

Our eyes both gravitate to the stunning emerald on her finger. "I still can't quite believe you're mine, you know," I murmur.

Gripping her hips, I lift her up onto the dresser, spreading her legs wide as I stare at her naked pussy. Her glistening pink slit is already swollen as I dig in, licking and sucking as if I'm starving – which I always am, for her.

She gasps as I reach up to roll and pinch her nipples between my fingers, sucking and lapping at her pussy until she cries out, holding on firmly to my hair. Turning my head, I suck a faint line of bite marks along her inner thigh. "Marking your territory?" she moans breathlessly.

"Yes – wait, no. I'm making art. You can judge me on it later."

Olivia begins to laugh, until my tongue delves deep and her laugh turns to a whimper. Her soft noises make my cock hard as stone as I tease her, swirling my tongue around her clit before thrusting deep again. Her thighs tighten around my shoulders as she moans louder, hips already rolling with need.

I devour her soft, wet pussy hungrily, growling and humming against her skin so she can feel the vibrations. Then I flatten my tongue across her clit, digging my fingers into her hips as I give her ass that familiar little shake that she loves so much.

"Please..." she begs, squirming with pleasure. Her warm, wet pussy is starting to drip, and I feel her stomach tense. "Yes...oh, yes..." she cries, twitching and moaning as her body dances for me. Her climax is always so beautiful, as I stare in awe while she shakes in bliss.

Holding her safely with one hand, I use the other to unfasten my belt, dropping my pants and stepping out of them. Then I pick her up and pin her against the one blank wall of the closet before shrugging off my shirt.

She gasps as my thick, throbbing cock presses against her soaking pussy. She's already trying to pull me in as I hold her just a bit too high for us to line up. "Please," she begs.

"Please, *what*?" It's taking all of my self-control to stop myself from impaling her hard on my cock, but I love watching the saucy light in her eyes.

"Please...fuck me, husband?"

My swollen head slicks back and forth through her slit, not quite dipping inside. "Ohh, I'm not sure you really want it."

"*Please*," she begs, staring into my eyes. "Take me hard. We both want it."

With one motion, I drive in, right to the hilt. Olivia screams in delight, her arms around my shoulders as she wriggles against me. Her tight, wet pussy always feels perfect.

Somewhere, on one of the dozens of beaches we visited over our honeymoon, I had an epiphany. I know now why I could never settle down before. It wasn't just my fear of repeating my father's mistakes. My fear of missing opportunities, or of being tied down.

I was searching for Olivia. And now that I've found her, my home is in her arms, in her sexy soft body, in her eyes.

My cock pounds deep and fast as her back squirms against the wall, her frantic moans muffled by my mouth. Our tongues dance together as her fingernails prick the back of my neck. I can already feel her inner walls tensing and rippling around me as I ram her deep, her breasts bouncing against my chest with every stroke.

Time seems to stop as we move together, moaning and thrusting and gasping and fucking...loving each other into oblivion. Reaching up to the back of her neck, I grip her hair hard, giving her head a gentle tug back as I stare into her eyes. "Come for your husband. Now."

With a twisted, savage moan, she obeys. Her body detonates, squirming and writhing as she explodes all around me, her pussy gripping me so tight that I have no choice but to come with her. Burying my cock deep, my mouth crashes to hers as long bursts of come spill inside her pussy.

We hold each other tightly for a long time, then she smiles, grinning widely. "I swear, the *one time* I do my hair nicely..."

"It's fine." She kisses me again, then I laugh as I look around. "I think this was probably the only room we hadn't fucked in yet."

She stares past my shoulder, thinking. "We still have the pantry. And the laundry room. Can't forget those."

Setting Olivia down on her feet, I grab her ass hard, pulling her against me. "We do love our tiny enclosed spaces, don't we?"

Her eyes blaze. "As long as I'm in your arms, you can take me anywhere you want."

Tucking her against my chest, we just hold each other quietly for several moments.

My sweet, gorgeous wife is starting the first job of her dream career next week. Our wonderful home is finished, except for a few beds in the garden. I adore my job as a pilot for the fastest-growing private airline in the country.

Right now, our lives have absolutely zero turbulence, except when we're endlessly rolling in the sheets.

Nothing but clear skies and endless love ahead.

If you haven't yet read *Rescued by the Surly Woodsman*, click here.

You'll meet Jace again in *Found by the Surly Ranger*, coming in June 2024.

The dining room is beautiful and timeless, with dark wooden ceiling beams, chandeliers, antique furniture, and a huge stone fireplace opposite a window that overlooks the forest and mountain. It takes a while for me to pull the rest of the tables slightly out of the way so that the one closest to the fire is obviously the special spot.

Once the table is set, I find the largest, sturdiest chairs, and start lugging the first into position.

"Hang on, let me help you."

The deep voice makes me jump, and I spin to stare into warm brown eyes that...oh my...

My breath and heart begin to sputter. He's...*gorgeous*.

"Damn, I'm sorry." He takes my elbow and sits me in the chair. "I think I scared you half to death."

The man is huge. Not like a bodybuilder; like a man who spends a lot of time swinging an axe. His dark green flannel shirt is just snug enough to show off his wide chest, and the sleeves are rolled up, showing off thick, tanned forearms and a bit of a dark, swirling tattoo.

Focus. You're here to serve him, and make his stay special.

"You're up early." I manage a soft laugh. "I heard you gentlemen got in quite late."

He chuckles, easily moving the other two chairs into place. I laugh as he lifts the last one with me still in it, setting it in position. "Nothing keeps me from good coffee."

I stand slowly, noticing the top of my head is barely at his shoulder. The man's nearly a foot taller than me. Looking up at his sculpted jawline and ruggedly handsome features, I can already tell it's going to be challenging to keep my focus.

"I'm Maya. I'll be your server this week."

"Nice to meet you, Maya. I'm Dylan. I'll be your guest asking for too much coffee."

Before I can reach for the coffee to pour, he serves himself. Then he notices my look of confusion. "Sorry. We're do-it-yourselfer types. Not used to being waited on. Hope that isn't annoying to you."

How could I be annoyed with a man like this looking so deeply into my eyes?

A bell rings faintly from the kitchen. "I'm guessing that fresh fruit and muffins with the coffee will be a good start before the full breakfast?"

Dylan sinks into a chair, his inviting lips pulled into a saucy grin. "I will eat everything you tell me to, Maya."

With a quick nod, I dash to the kitchen, replaying what he just said. Oh my... Was he *flirting*? Did he mean for that to sound so racy?

My cheeks flame as I gather the trays. I'm going to have to be very careful that Dylan and I are never alone again.

I don't think my heart can take it.

Don't worry, Maya's heart is going to be just fine in *Thin Ice – Winter Heat at Wolfe Mountain.*

ALSO BY HALEY TRAVIS

Book links at haleytravisromance.com

Thin Ice - Winter Heat at Wolfe Mountain Chalet

He's a total stranger. Until I slip and fall into his arms, and then into his bed.

He claims he's a loner, but that doesn't explain why he's obsessed with me. Yet from the second he growls, "You're mine," into my ear, I want it to be true.

The Lumberjack's Quirky Girl

I probably shouldn't have ogled Braden Oakley's big axe. *Oops.*

Tall as a redwood and built like a moose, the devastatingly gorgeous lumberjack should have nothing in common with little miss artsy-pants—aka, *me*. So how come the harder I try to stay away, the more I end up wrapped up in his muscled arms begging for more of his hard…wood?

Meet all four HOT Oakley brothers HERE.

Possessing My Lily

From the second her delicate body thumped into my chest, I knew Lily was mine.

Every detail of my gorgeous, sweet girl is precious. Yet she's sensitive, and doesn't trust that we're already together. I'll find a way to prove I'm worth getting through her fears. That my possession will be the best thing for both of us.

<u>Her New Bodyguard: Jackson</u>

It was supposed to be a simple personal security job. But Ashley was so sexy and innocent that my need to care for her was far more than professional.

Mackton Mechanics

Rev your engines and get ready to fall for these hot mechanics! These huge, rough men are comfortable working with steel. What will happen when they're tinkering with a sweet girl's heart instead of a motor?

Fake Summer Wife

I'd always been too timid. But when a gorgeous man needed a favor and asked me out in front of the whole diner, I had to say yes... I would be his phony wife for one night.

For new release updates from Amazon, go to the author's page, then click **+Follow** near the top left.

Please join the mailing list at haleytravisromance.com for new releases, updates, discounts & freebies!